I0712918

COSCOM
ENTERTAINMENT

ALSO BY A.P. FUCHS

BLOOD OF MY WORLD TRILOGY

DISCOVERY OF DEATH
MEMORIES OF DEATH
LIFE OF DEATH

UNDEAD WORLD TRILOGY

BLOOD OF THE DEAD
POSSESSION OF THE DEAD

THE AXIOM-MAN™ SAGA
(LISTED IN READING ORDER)

AXIOM-MAN
EPISODE NO. 0: FIRST NIGHT OUT
DOORWAY OF DARKNESS
EPISODE NO. 1: THE DEAD LAND
CITY OF RUIN
OF MAGIC AND MEN (COMIC BOOK)

OTHER FICTION

A STRANGER DEAD
A RED DARK NIGHT
APRIL (WRITING AS PETER FOX)
MAGIC MAN (DELUXE CHAPBOOK)
THE WAY OF THE FOG (THE ARK OF LIGHT VOL. 1)
DEVIL'S PLAYGROUND (WRITTEN WITH KEITH GOUVEIA)
ON HELL'S WINGS (WRITTEN WITH KEITH GOUVEIA)
ZOMBIE FIGHT NIGHT: BATTLES OF THE DEAD
MAGIC MAN PLUS 15 TALES OF TERROR
UNDENIABLE

Anthologies (as Editor)

Dead Science
Elements of the Fantastic
Vicious Verses and Reanimated Rhymes: Zany
Zombie Poetry for the Undead Head
Metahumans vs the Undead

Non-fiction

Book Marketing for the
Financially-challenged Author

Poetry

The Hand I've Been Dealt
Haunted Melodies and Other Dark Poems
Still About A Girl

Go to

www.canisterx.com

&

www.undeadworldtrilogy.com

A RED DARK NIGHT

A.P. FUCHS

COSCOM ENTERTAINMENT
WINNIPEG

ISBN 978-1-926712-90-1

Published by COSCOM ENTERTAINMENT
www.coscomentertainment.com
Text set in Garamond; Printed and bound in the USA

COVER ART BY C.J. HUTCHINSON AND
JESUS MORALES/DARK RIDDLE

For M. Jane Letty
You give me hope
Bless you

Inside the Veil

It Started With B-Movies
Introduction by the Author

A RED DARK *Night* started out as an attempt to just do a simple B-horror novel, the kind that takes place at a summer camp, some kind of monster is on the loose, a bunch of beautiful girls are the targets, and the whole thing ends in a bloodbath.

Simple premise. Simple idea. Just need to buckle down and write it out. And I did. I started this book during work hours at a call centre job I once held, then finished it a short while later at home. However, the task of writing what was supposed to be a simple story turned into something far more complex. I did the worst thing any writer could do and that was write themselves into a corner. I won't say how I did it and spoil the book for you, but I basically got to a point where the story stopped and I was stuck with a partially-finished book. Not believing in trunk novels—those books, partial or complete, most writers have that they've written but never see the light of day—I took a short break from *A Red Dark Night* to see if a solution would present itself. Sure enough, it was a short period until one came. It was a risk, something that would turn what was supposed to be a very basic B-horror story on its ear. But it was the only way the book could proceed.

A Red Dark Night was completed in 2003 (I think) and published as the first novel through my company, Coscom Entertainment, in 2004. The reviews were positive and, at the time, it sold not bad for a small press book. Nothing terrible, but nothing to brag about either.

Regardless, this book is a special story to me because it represents my fourth effort at writing a novel, one written a short few years into my career, and carries the voice of a young writer with bright-eyed hope for the future.

As my career progressed and Coscom Entertainment grew into a respectable publishing house, I decided to pull *A Red Dark Night* from the market. Not because it was a bad book, but simply because I wanted to tweak the writing of what is to me one of the most favorite stories I've ever written. I wanted to give you, dear reader, the best version of it I could.

That's what this book is: the best version of *A Red Dark Night*. I didn't go back and overhaul the whole thing and knockout the voice of the kid who wrote it, but I did clean it up and made it read better while still maintaining the original voice of a young man with a love for B-movies.

Revisiting this book, for me, after so long was bittersweet. It reminded me of what life used to be like before I grew up, the simple life of just working a day job and writing stories in the evening. That was pretty much all I did. It was a way to visit a young man in the past and rediscover what he was thinking and what he had to say.

I hope as you read this you'll see the passion behind the words of this story and my love of B-horror, as well as see how the imagination was really allowed to run wild without the pressures of everyday life.

To be a kid again . . . let's do that now, together, and sit around the campfire as I share with you a story about strange creatures that lurk in the woods.

- A.P. Fuchs
Winnipeg, MB
July 31, 2011

A RED DARK NIGHT

Prologue
In 1982

THE SHEETS ON the bed stirred as something slithered beneath them.

Shelly couldn't move. Her prone body ached with apprehension—a dull pulse of fear. She wasn't sure what was beneath the cotton fabric, but she was certain it was thin, flat and incredibly long; wet like a warm sponge and smooth like ivory. The very *feel* of it against her skin between her legs made her lower back tense with unease.

She briefly glanced around at the other girls on the bunk beds in the small cabin. They all appeared to be asleep in perfect slumber. No one moved.

The long wet thing between the sheets snaked along the inside of her thighs. Her nightgown was bunched up around her hips from tossing and turning earlier as she tried to fall asleep. Her hands trembling, she wanted so badly to push her nightgown down, to cover her legs, but she dare not; if she did, she would touch that wet mess of whatever it was between her legs with her fingers. A mental flash of the wet thing jumping out of the sheets and latching onto her made her stomach do a flip.

She briefly considered it might be her period coming on early. Yet, she wasn't due for another few days, and there was far too much wetness to count as normal menstrual leakage. She knew she hadn't wet herself either. If she had, it would have pooled in a large circle between her legs and wouldn't be trickling *horizontally* along her thighs. Vertically, maybe, but not lengthwise. Liquid didn't move by itself and it especially wouldn't move toward her instead of away.

Pale moonlight came in from the window on the far side of the wood-paneled room. The door was behind her and she felt the cool night breeze blowing in from the crack underneath where the door met the wooden floorboards.

What was between her legs?

It slithered again, brushing against the inside of her right thigh near her groin, and then moved swiftly over to the left, licking her other leg. Fingers trembling, Shelly gripped the starched, white fabric of the bedsheet; the sweat off her palms quickly soaked into the material. Her mouth was dry and when she swallowed, the back of her throat pinched with discomfort.

Get it together. Squeeze and pull. You can't lie here all night. Her thoughts lingered in her head like a sad memory. She closed her eyes and breathed slowly, centering herself. She gripped the bedsheet and . . . lifted. At least, she thought she did. When she opened her eyes, she saw instead the sheet remained flat, completely covering her. She hadn't lifted the blanket after all and the moisture brushing the inside of her legs grew even wetter, drew even closer.

Lift or let this thing get you! She hated herself for not tossing the sheet back the first time.

With a new surge of strength, her heart pulsing in rapid aches, she tore the bedsheet up and over to the side, close to the wall against her bed.

On impulse, her body shot up, sitting, her bottom scooting back closer to her pillow, her arms and legs shaking. She wanted to yelp, to make any kind of noise, but no sound would come. Her voice stopped at the top of her neck, thumping against her trachea as though banging against a roof.

In the moonlight between her legs sat a long ribbon of darkness. The thick goo was like syrup, and when it rippled, the moonlight reflecting off its surface revealed its deep red color.

The goo seemed to . . . be alive, peering up at her questioningly, as if asking her why she removed the bedsheet. Shelly stared back, her spine locking up in intense apprehension for what might happen next.

It's . . . it's . . . The thoughts could not form; *would* not form. She couldn't believe this thick strip of goo—this long puddle that looked like blood—was truly looking up at her. It had no eyes but there was something . . . . It *was* looking at her. She was certain of it.

Finally, her voice plowed through the imaginary roof in her throat and her shrill scream woke the other girls in the cabin. They all sat up with a start and looked quickly to Shelly sitting upright, screeching on her bed.

Shelly briefly glanced up at the others. They all stared down at her—nine other campers and their counselor— eyes wide and mouths agape. One of the girls, Mary, had her face hidden in her hands, her brown hair coiled between her fingers.

Facing the goo between her legs, Shelly gasped when she saw it swirl, gathering itself in a glimmering, liquid mound of deep red between her legs.

She screamed when the liquid, seeming to have quadrupled in size, pounced upon her and completely covered her in a silky wave.

Beneath the blanket of the red goo and only dimly aware of what was happening around her, Shelly couldn't tell if she was still sitting up or if she had been thrown down and forced to lie there. The liquid sloshed around her, as though she was either underwater or in a bathtub. Moving was thick and slow-going like trying to wade through Jell-O. Then, as if her skin had been licked with flame, she felt her flesh begin to tear and peel as something tried to crawl under her skin. Worse, she knew what that *something* was. The red goo was seeping into her, contaminating her, filling her. *Sinking* into her.

All of a sudden, there was a low thumping, like a deep beat on wood. The thumping persisted, growing louder and louder, like a bass drum in the distance coming closer, then—it stopped. The loud tear of what sounded like a rag being ripped in two filled her ears. She shuddered.

A loud bang blew up in her insides, its sound echoing through everything that she was, through her flesh, bones and more. The red goo screeched, and then suddenly flew off like a blanket being snatched up by its middle and was tossed away.

The sounds around her were now clear and crisp: girls screaming, the counselor included, her pitch slightly lower than the others'; Mary crying; sharp, low footsteps on the cabin's wooden floor.

The red goo screeched and growled, a blob of red sloshing against the air as though in an upright tub.

All the girls' eyes were on the door. Shelly, realizing she was still sitting up, turned around swiftly on her bottom, following their gaze. And then, standing in the doorway, was a large man in a loose-fitting white shirt not of this century, his brown trousers clinging to his thighs as though tights, his leg muscles a bulge of steel through the material. His hair sat atop his head in long brown waves. A long velvet black cape hung over his shoulders, its leather strap across his chest, and its hem down to the ankles of his brown folded-over boots. His blue-eyed gaze was as cold as freezing rain and as firm as iron. He stared down his muscular arm, focusing on the gleaming silver gauntlet attached to his forearm. Smoke trailed out of the gauntlet's end, where the tip gathered in a point. The door lay in splinters at his feet.

Like lightning, the red goo dove over Shelly's bed in a brilliant arc of crimson, splashing as it hit the floorboards, and then slowly began pulling itself together again.

The girls continued their hysterical screams; all except for Mary. She just sat there on her top bunk, legs crossed, face in her hands, her long brown bangs hanging over her fingers, crying.

The red puddle coalesced into a thick blob and soon that blob began to grow taller and taller and taller. Slowly, it took on a humanlike form. It looked like a man made from hard candy, red and semi-transparent. It was male in shape and muscle structure, but that was all; there were no eyes, ears, nose, mouth or cheek, just red goo in the shape of a man.

Buzzing filled the air and Shelly realized it was coming from the man in the cape's gauntlet, as though the silver weapon were powering itself up. At least that's what it sounded like. The red-man charged toward the man in the cape and within the space of a second another bright blue fireball shot at the creature, causing it to spray in all directions.

This time, the red goo didn't reassemble.

"One for warning, two for glory," the man in the cape said.

He eyed the screaming girls one by one, his blue eyes carrying the weight of disappointment, as though these girls had just seen something they were never meant to. He turned and left the cabin, his black cape concealing him as he disappeared into the night.

It was a long while before the girls were able to silence their screeching tongues.

Chapter One
Today

Mary Thompson led Doug Melky down the old leafy trail that circled around Camp Silverway. She was thirty-seven and this was her second year back at camp since the summer of '82. After that one night in the cabin, after seeing that red . . . thing . . . wrap itself around Shelly, going back to Camp Silverway was never an option. Now, so many years later, she had to come back. It wasn't her choice to begin with, but rather that of her psychiatrist, Dr. Woodrose, at Hans Memorial Hospital. He told her eventually she would have to face her fears, her haunting memories, and revisit the dark time in her past when things went haywire. This was last year. When Mary returned, she was surprised to see Camp Silverway nearly identical to how she remembered it when she was fifteen.

The sign, mounted on a large arch over the entrance, proudly read CAMP SILVERWAY. The camp ran along a dirt road off the highway, the camp bordering a lake. The cabins for the campers bordered a ring of bushes and trees that wrapped around the open clearing of the camp like a horseshoe. At the opening of the horseshoe was the lake, with a long cedar wood dock running from the sandy canoe-lined shore out into the water where campers went waterskiing. At the center of the camp stood the lodge which served as both mess hall and indoor activity and meeting centre. Other activity centres, like the climbing wall, were scattered about the camp; some concealed in the bushes, others out in the open.

Now Mary was back again. Last year she signed on as a camp counselor, hoping to come to grips with her fear.

Despite all trepidations over going back to Camp Silverway, last summer was a fine one spent looking after ten fifteen-year-old girls in Cabin Six. She was thankful to have been assigned to that cabin; that terrible summer in '82 was spent in Cabin Seven and spending a night in there would have been more than she could handle. But she did find herself peering out the window at the aging, rustic structure more than once while the girls slept. She envisioned Cabin Seven's interior, the bunk bed up against the wall where Shelly once slept. Although she spent most of that horrible night with her face in her hands, she remembered peering between her fingers, watching as the red goo slithered and snaked over Shelly's body, forming itself to and over her friend like some kind of red plastic food wrap.

On these nights when she eyed Cabin Seven, sometimes she stared at just the door, knowing full well it was replaced after the mysterious man in the velvet black cape kicked it down. The morning after, when the camp counselors at the time inspected the door and the girls told of the strange man who shot fire from his hands and kicked the door open, many of the counselors took the tale as nothing more than a far-fetched yarn. Even so, when the Royal Canadian Mounted Police came by, they searched in a twenty-kilometer radius around the camp, looking for the supposed mystery man. He never turned up. Soon, the story of his arrival at the cabin faded to a tale told around campfires before bedtime, then eventually faded away altogether.

Mary tugged Doug's hand, leading him off a leafy trail and into the bushes. There was a small clearing around here somewhere, she remembered. After walking a few moments, parting the thin branches of the high bushes and stepping around the trees, Mary rose on her tiptoes. She spotted the clearing, just over to the right.

"Come on," she said as she gave his hand another tug.

"You sure about this? Don't you think we'll get caught?" he said.

"You kidding? Everyone's inside the lodge for lunch. No one'll be out for another half-hour, forty-five minutes."

"If you say so."

She knew full well Doug wasn't supposed to be there with her. Camp Silverway had an unwritten rule of no boys allowed.

Walking backwards, facing him, his hand still in hers, she gave him a sly and seductive grin. Soon enough, they were in the clearing. Mary watched as he took in her long brown hair blowing in the subtle breeze.

The moment they were in the center of the clearing, she took one last look around. Seeing the coast was clear, she dove at Doug, nearly tackling him to the ground, his face in her hands as she passionately kissed him. His hands gripped her about the waist, squeezing her, occasionally tugging the fabric of her tight white Camp Silverway T-shirt. His hands ran down her snug-fitting blue shorts, his fingers grazing over her bottom, sending electricity throughout her body.

She pawed at his green tank top and stuck her hands under it, feeling the smooth hardness of his chest. He wasn't a big man but he was fit, more than other men of his size. He wore blue jeans. She promptly rolled back onto her knees, dragging him up with her.

"Doug . . ." she said, her voice soft, almost catching in her throat. His touch was soothing, calming, and yet strong enough to drive pleasure through her like a wind through a screen door.

It wasn't long until she had her panties and shorts by her ankles and was only wearing her bra and socks. Doug stripped down completely.

"Gently," she breathed.

"I love you," he whispered into her ear.

She tried to speak, but no words came.

Her eyes still closed, she gave herself to him, true, passionate, intimate. She lost herself in the moment.

Doug groaned then screamed as hot liquid splashed against Mary's skin. Her eyes shot open and she screeched. He hung over her, covered in blood.

Then there was no sound, as if she became suddenly deaf.

Heart racing, she watched as Doug's body upper teetered over her, like a marionette that lost its puppet master. A suctioning slurp filled her ears as sound suddenly returned. She peered around his body and screamed again when she saw red goo pulsating on his back.

She tried to get to her feet, but Doug's weight atop her thighs was too much for her rubbery legs. She pushed against him hard, her palms immediately soaked with the blood on his chest. His crimson form toppled backward, landing on top of the red slime sucking on his back. Mary scrambled to her feet but the moment she tried to run, she tripped over the blood-stained blue shorts around her ankles. Not caring she was naked save for her now red-with-blood bra and socks, she ripped the shorts and panties away and got to her feet. She tore off into the forest, fighting to get away from whatever it was that had Doug.

The trees and bushes rushed by her in a blur of green. From behind, she heard a low growl followed by a foul screech along with the parting of bushes and crunching of leaves.

It was following her.

Mary darted left then right then left again, trying desperately to throw whatever was pursuing her off her trail. She glanced over her shoulder and saw a flash of liquid crimson against the sharp green of leaves. For some reason she briefly thought of Christmas, but this was no merry time. She pushed on.

The forest around her all looked the same: nothing but trees and bush. It was only after she tripped over an unearthed root and came crashing to the ground did she realize she was running *away* from the camp instead of toward it. Scrambling to her feet, Mary turned sharply to the right and ran quite a ways before heading back in the direction of where she thought the camp was.

Come on. Let's go! Even just thinking was a challenge as all her energy was being poured into her legs; her thighs and calves already burned from their exertion.

There was another growl off to her right, sounding this time more like a panther hatefully calling at its prey.

The thin branches from the higher bushes slapped across her chest, a few leaving red slash marks across the tops of her breasts. She stepped on something sharp and she briefly thought of a pointed twig or the tip of a rough branch poking through her sock and into her skin.

Up ahead . . . was that . . . was it . . . a clearing? Were the trees and bushes getting thinner?

There was the rumble of what sounded like horse hooves behind her, the ground shaking from its fast beat.

Run!

Focusing herself, she dug her heels hard into the ground, ignoring how painful running on the harsh forest floor was in only socks.

When she came out of the forest, the main clearing of Camp Silverway was off to her right.

She sprinted for the lodge.

Chapter Two
Tarek

T HE CAMP'S LODGE was fast approaching.

As a cramp suddenly shot through Mary's left leg, her pace immediately slowed to a brisk trot.

"Gruhh!" She was limping now and the sudden realization of her nakedness made her uncomfortable and ashamed. "Help! Someone, anyone, help!"

Through the windows she saw people sitting in the mess hall inside the lodge, going about their business, paying no mind to the half-naked, blood-splattered girl hobbling their way as fast as she was able.

Just as she was about to round to the front of the building, a loud growl filled the air and a red, humanlike form bounded out of the woods, clearing the bush-tops by at least ten feet, arms and legs splayed out like a bird in flight. It landed like a raindrop splashing onto the pavement. The red puddle then returned to its humanlike form and darted toward her.

Mary screamed; behind her she heard the movement of chairs scraping against the wooden floor inside the mess hall. She sensed the young female faces filling the windows.

The red manlike thing was before her in no time, its body in midair, its arms outstretched, its hands forming into pincers, ready to tear her head off. Then . . .

The roar of fire filled her ears as a ball of blue light swept past her head. Her hair crackled, the flame grazing her just above her ears. The fireball hit the creature square on, sending it tumbling back and onto the grass in a puddle. No sooner did it splash out everywhere did it begin to reform itself back into a featureless man.

Mary glanced up over her shoulder. On the lodge's roof was a man in a black velvet cape. There was something familiar about him.

The creature, now humanlike again, spiraled through the air toward Mary. There was the thud of boots hitting the ground and a higher-pitched mechanical sound as the gleaming, silver gauntlet on the man's forearm powered up. A ball of light more brilliant than the first spewed forth from the gauntlet's pointed end and cleanly sliced the head off the creature's body. The headless, red form teetered back and forth before falling to the ground in another splash.

It was over.

Mary collapsed to her knees and buried her face in her hands. Her sweaty, blood-spattered brown hair hung loosely over her fingers.

This was all too familiar.

Years had been spent in a psychiatrist's office, convincing herself that what happened in the summer of '82 hadn't been real.

But it was happening again.

The campers and counselors poured out of the lodge's front doors, and then rounded to the back of the building where Mary was on her knees with the man in the black cape standing by her.

"What is that?" one of the girls said, pointing to the blood pool on the ground.

There were murmurs throughout the crowd, but most stood in awe looking at the pile of red goo coating the grass.

Tears welling in her eyes, Mary stood, and when she wiped her tears away, she saw everyone's gaze had shifted to the man in the black cape. His muscular arm was still held out, his gauntlet pointed at the red slime. When he saw Mary looking his way, he slowly lowered his arm, tucking it in behind the large folds of his cape. His deep blue eyes set upon her from behind long, brown bangs of wavy hair.

She knew who this man was: the same man that had rescued the girls in Cabin Seven so long ago. Now, looking at him, she saw he hadn't aged a day. *How could that*—But before she could finish her thought, the man turned away and walked toward the other campers. They parted as he made his way past, their eyes remaining upon him.

"Wait!" Mary called out and all eyes turned her way. A few of the girls smiled; one giggled.

The man turned, the billows of his white shirt rippling as he moved. Mary came over to him.

"Yes?" he said, his voice as smooth as ivory yet carrying the backbone of pain. Perhaps loss.

I can't even remember what I wanted to say, she thought as a subtle breeze swept between them and goose bumps formed on her exposed skin.

The man looked her up and down, paying no mind to the things a man would find attractive about a half-naked woman.

"I'm sorry," he said. "Here." He undid the leather strap across his chest, letting the cape fall to one side. He wrapped the cloak around her and tugged it snug around her neck.

"Thank you," she said.

There were more murmurs in the crowd.

He grinned sweetly, and then brought his gauntleted forearm up to his chest and gazed at it as if appraising a rare antique.

"You never saw me," he said and walked away.

"Your name," she called. *What's—* "—your name?"

The man kept walking and she didn't think he was going to answer. Then, still focused forward, he said, "Tarek," sounding as if he *had* to say his name as opposed to wanting to say it.

Mary turned toward the other girls. They came running to her like a swarm of bees over a flower, asking her if she was all right or if there was anything they could get her. All she could think about was Tarek. She hugged his cape closer.

Most of the girls were with Mary inside the mess hall. Some were elsewhere in the camp, as they had finished their lunch before Mary's arrival with the blood-like creature and the appearance of Tarek, and had gone off to their next activity for the afternoon.

She sat at one of the ten round lacquered tables, Tarek's cape still wrapped around her shoulders. One of the other counselors came into the room with a bundle of clothing in her arms.

"Here," Becky said. "Put these on."

Mary didn't acknowledge her. There was nothing *to* acknowledge. She was still lost in the memory of moments prior, that blood-like creature lunging at her, the one that had killed Doug. His death was still fresh; it was hard to believe he was actually gone. Her heart ached and tears leaked from the corners of her eyes. And Tarek. *You never saw me,* Tarek said. However, she *had* seen him, seen him shoot that blue fire from the silver gauntlet on his right forearm as though he was hurling a baseball.

"Tarek," she whispered.

None of the girls seemed to have heard her. She glanced at the clothing Becky put on the table. A white T-shirt with CAMP SILVERWAY written across its front in gray letters, and a pair of jeans. Becky and Mary were similar in size so the jeans would fit with no problem. She also brought her a pair of white socks and a pair of sneakers from the cabinet by the door, where shoes used for those who forgot their own sneakers at home sat in disarray.

"Thank you," Mary said.

Becky's hazel eyes were warm and comforting. "Sure," she said as she rubbed Mary's back.

Mary gathered up the clothing and went to the kitchen that ran off the mess hall to change. When she returned, she had Tarek's black cape folded over one forearm.

"Who was that guy?" one of the girls asked while being met with a *Shush* from another.

I don't know who he was, Helen, Mary thought. Helen. One of the girls in Mary's cabin. Cabin Six.

"I'm not sure," Mary said.

"Well, whoever he was," Helen said, "he was . . . weird." She glanced around at the others. "Did you see that thing he had on his arm? That thing that shot fire? Man, strange. What's worse was that thing he shot the fire *at*. I've never seen anything like it. It wasn't human, whatever that red thing was. Craziness, I tell you."

"What do you mean 'not human'?" another one of the girls, Tara, said.

Helen turned to her. "You tell me the last time you saw a pile of walking red goo that looked human. It was like a moving statue made of Jell-O."

Tara didn't say anything.

"Whatever it was," Mary said, "I hope it doesn't return." *It can't. I wouldn't be able to handle it. It's just like that summer, like that thing that covered Shelly.* Tears welled up in her eyes.

Becky put her arms around Mary. "It'll be okay," she said.

Mary fell into her arms and hugged her tight, sobbing into her shoulder. *I hope it will. I hope.*

It started about mid afternoon. Only Mary and Becky were in the mess hall, the rest of the girls having gone to call their parents for pickup later that day.

"It's not safe here," Becky had told them. "You should all go home. Camp fees will be reimbursed accordingly once all this is settled."

Some were sad to go, but others welcomed it. They didn't want to be anywhere near camp should another of those blood-like men—creatures, whatever it was— returned.

"I can't stop thinking about it," Mary said. "I thought it was all in my head. Well, I convinced myself it was, anyway. But what happened to Shelly . . . it was real. It *actually* happened. It happened to Doug. My sweet Doug. And now it's happening again. Happening to *me.*" She rested her chin on her hands, elbows on the table. Becky sat across from her, arms folded, legs crossed.

There was a long quiet moment before Becky said anything. "Was it . . . was that thing the same as, you know, the same as the one that came in '82?"

"I don't know. Probably." She took a deep breath. "Then again, now you've just made me think there might be more than one." A shudder ran through her. "I hate thinking about it."

"Yeah, well—" Becky stopped, her eyes staring at the window. "What is that?" she whispered.

She got up and went to the window overlooking the grassy area where Mary, the creature, and Tarek had been earlier.

"Mary, come look at this." She waved her over.

Mary slowly got up, the legs of her chair scraping against the hardwood floor of the mess hall. "What?" she asked once she was beside Becky.

"There."

Becky pointed out to the edge where the forest met the grass, to the spaces in between the cabins. A dark strip about a foot wide ran along the bottom edge of the trees.

"What? It's just a shadow," Mary said.

Becky squinted. Mary put her tongue between her teeth, a habit of hers when she wasn't sure of something.

"I don't think so," Becky said after a time.

Mary took a closer look. Her heart leaped in her chest when she saw the shadow had a red tinge. Was it her imagination or had the shadow, just this instant, grown wider, as though coming toward them? Worse, was it now thicker, like a fog floating along the ground? She didn't think so. Yet . . .

There was no mistaking it. It wasn't a shadow. Shadows weren't blood-red.

They came out of the lodge together, Becky walking in front of Mary. They stepped slowly toward the dark red shadow on the ground. Out under the bright afternoon sun, the shadow's redness was more apparent, almost cherry-colored.

With her thoughts running a mile a minute, Mary recognized the red hue was the same as that of the creature.

Tarek. The name came out of nowhere. Then, intentionally thinking of the man in the old-fashioned white shirt and brown trousers, *Help*. That's all she could think. Nothing more would come.

Over five inches up and down and two feet wide, the shadow rippled on the ground like subtle waves on a morning lake. Nothing held the dark red liquid in place; it held its form all by itself.

Off in the trees, something moved.

Mary peered closer at the forest while Becky still had her eyes on the shadow.

The bright green of the leaves rustled with the wind, the trees swaying gently toward Mary.

There was suddenly another flash of red in the forest, running like a sprinter behind a tattered green veil.

Mary touched Becky's arm and she gave a start.

"It's moving," Becky said still looking at the shadow. "That's impossible."

Mary gave Becky's short sleeve a tug. "The woods. Something's out there."

Becky looked at the trees. Dotted in behind the leaves in a line as far to the right and left as Mary could see, were red forms: faceless humanlike shapes, masculine in structure, looking their way.

"Let's get inside," Mary nearly shouted.

"Good idea."

When the two women turned about to go back to the lodge, they both shrieked as a blood-like creature slithered along the ground toward them like a stream through cracks in the pavement. They screamed even louder when the puddle took on the form of a man, featureless save for the musculature of his body.

The creature lunged at them, going straight for Mary, its newly-formed arms held out, ready to clamp around her neck.

The strength ran from Mary's legs and she collapsed. Lying on her back, she watched as the creature changed direction in midair and dove toward Becky. It splashed against her like a water balloon against a wall, pushing her backward, her legs trapped under her.

"Becky!" Mary said, getting to her feet as quickly as possible.

The creature writhed and squirmed over Becky's body, seeming to soak into her. Because it was semi-transparent, Mary saw through the dark, murky red of the creature's body straight to Becky underneath. Her friend's mouth was open in a scream. No sound came. The creature seeped into her like water being sucked up by a sponge.

That *powering-up* sound fell on the air, starting off quiet then building in intensity and strength.

Tarek had returned.

Before Mary realized what happened, Tarek stood over Becky's limp body, the creature moving over and into her in gel-like ripples.

"Is she . . . is she . . ." Mary wanted to ask him if her friend was alive, but her voice caught in her throat.

"Get back." Tarek's voice was like thunder during a calm afternoon.

Mary obeyed and stepped backward, nearly tripping over her own feet. She glanced at the trees. The other creatures were gone.

Tarek aimed his gauntlet at the creature, its silver casing sparkling in the sunlight.

In a blast of heat, a fireball roared out of the gauntlet's end and encompassed both Becky and the creature in a net of flame. He then jumped back a step and shot another ball of fire at the creature.

A shrieking squeal filled the air, like a rat burning alive.

After a time of eternal screeching and screaming, the creature's sound stopped and lay still atop Becky, half soaked into her body, half not.

With a look of finality in his icy-blue eyes, Tarek turned to Mary.

"It is finished," he said.

Finished? What's fin— "What was it?" Mary asked. *Becky!* "She's . . . she's . . ."

"She's gone. For now, anyway," Tarek said as he walked away from her.

"Wait!" Mary ran after him, grabbed his arm and spun him around. She got the distinct feeling that should he have chose, he could have resisted her. "I . . . I can't believe she's—" She glanced back at Becky's brick-red-goo-stained body. Tears filled her eyes. "Hold me."

As Tarek took her into his arms, Mary wept.

Chapter Three

Bloodans

"YOU HAVE TO be honest with me," Mary said to Tarek, handing him back his cape. They were in the mess hall.

"I can't," he said as he clasped its silver buckle, joining the two ends of the leather strap across his chest. The hem of his cape fell to below his ankles.

Yes, you can. You have to, she thought. "I'm serious."

Finished fixing his cape in place, he lowered his hands, the silver gauntlet on the table beside them. "So am I." There was an iron coldness in his voice, one she never experienced before.

His shoulders settled as though a heavy beam stretched across them.

"You have to tell me what those things were."

The imaginary beam across his shoulders seemed to weigh down on him even more. She half-expected his legs to buckle under the weight.

"They shouldn't be here," he simply said.

Tell me something I don't know, she thought. She did her best to remain calm. She knew if she became forceful in her tone, he would most likely not tell her a thing.

"I was there when they . . . it . . . when one of them came the first time, twenty-two years ago," she said.

Raising an eyebrow, his blue eyes suddenly seemed to grow larger.

She continued. "Cabin Seven. Just over there." She nodded in its direction through the mess hall window. "You came and broke the door down and . . . it was on

Shelly. You drove it off her with the fire from your . . . your . . ." Her eyes rested on the gauntlet on the table.

"You were crying," he said.

"Yes."

"You had your face in your hands."

"Yes."

Tears swelled in her eyes at the memory. *He remembers me.*

"The sound a person makes when they cry doesn't change," he said. "It matures with their age but its *undercurrent* remains the same."

Mary sat and rested an elbow on the table. It was a long moment before she spoke. "Where are you from?"

Tarek turned away from her and adjusted his cape. "Some place far away, a long time from here."

"Long time?"

"Doesn't matter. Those creatures—Bloodans, they're called—are just what their name implies. Blood. That's what they're made of. Blood, evil and a darkness so black that even the depths of a moonless night sky pales in comparison."

"How—" There was really no right set of words that came to mind. "What are they really? How can something like that exist?"

Tarek turned back to her. "I told you what they are. However, they're not supposed to be here, no more than I."

"You said you are from a long time from here. What does that mean?" She wasn't sure she wanted to know but had to ask the question anyway.

"I don't want to say too much," he said. "I really don't. Listen, um—"

"—Mary."

"Mary. The less you know, the better. Once this is finished, I don't want you knowing too much about where I'm from and what I do. Worse, I don't want you knowing too much about the Bloodans. Knowing too much might . . . it might trigger their return again."

Their return? But what . . . what triggered their return this time? How— "How did they come here the first time? Back in '82?"

Tarek laid a large hand atop the shiny silver finish of the gauntlet. His fingers stroked it as though he was petting a cat. Then he picked it up from the table and fixed it onto his right forearm. "Bloodans," he began, "are made of blood. They come from a place where more has been shed than on any other ground on Earth. The evil which caused that bloodshed's very real. It is the embodiment of darkness, the essence of death and murder, and that evil gives them life. Death fuels them. Unfortunately, as long as there is death, there will be Bloodans."

Mary wasn't quite sure what he was saying. It barely made sense. "How many are there?" she asked. "How many Bloodans have, um, come back here?"

"As far as I'm aware, there was just the one that claimed your friend."

Becky. Her heart ached. Becky had been a good and close friend.

"But I saw more hiding in the forest," Mary said. The forest. Doug. Doug was dead. Mary quickly flashed back to him straddling her and that awful liquid-like creature clinging to his back like a leech. A chill swept through her and a sickening knot formed in her stomach. Her heart ached. *Doug . . .*

"More?" he said as he glanced away. There was a pause before he went on. "I'm sorry I didn't get there fast enough."

He's talking about Doug. "It's not your fault." *Or could you have saved him?* She didn't know. Who knew how soon Tarek, being wherever he was at the time Doug was attacked, was able to get to Camp Silverway and kill the creature?

Before she could ask how he knew to come for the creature, Tarek's head cocked to the side, as though listening to a sound only he could hear.

"What?" she asked.

"I have to go." There was something almost majestic about the way he moved as he spun around, his black cape billowing out, his silver gauntlet twinkling in the sunlight coming through the window.

It took only a moment for her to gather enough strength to follow.

Chapter Four
Two Girls

T HE LARGE BOAT shed next to the canoe racks by the lake had been there ever since the camp was built over thirty years ago. Every decade a new coat of paint was thrown on to match the times; a pale orange and muddy brown in the seventies; bad purples and pinks in the eighties; neon greens and yellows in the nineties; and reds and blues for the new millennium. The shed held all things needed for any aquatic activities that were part of the camp's program on any given year: water skis, life jackets, four kayaks, two kneeboards and one surfboard, as well as a spare onboard motor for one of the speedboats by the dock.

There was a clothesline outside the shed for wet towels and bathing suits, then next to the clothesline, a small changing house so the girls could switch from camp clothes to bathing suits without going all the way back to their cabins.

The boating shed was already closed for the day, all of the water activities done earlier that morning. No one was around.

Carla led Skyla by the hand around to the rear of the shed. The two girls, both with brown hair and gray eyes—a trait they shared and based their friendship on— crept up the side of the shed. Carla kept her eyes peeled for any onlookers. The two snuck off earlier that morning just after water-skiing, and if they got caught, odds were they'd have to spend the rest of the afternoon in their cabin.

They rounded the front of the boating shed and, taking one last look around for anyone who might be watching, undid the wooden latch that kept the two large swinging doors shut. Carla partially opened one of those doors and Skyla ducked under her arm and went in. Carla followed and, squeezing her fingers through the crack where the two doors met, put the latch back in place from the inside.

"Okay," Carla whispered, "you can pull it."

There was the light jingle of metal and then the *chink-chank* as Skyla pulled down on the thin chain that hooked to the light mounted over the door. The shed suddenly enveloped in the warm glow of light, the browns of the interior walls giving off the coziness of a ski-lodge.

"You don't think anyone will come, do you?" Skyla asked.

"No," Carla said. "Do you got them?"

Skyla pulled out two aerosol paint cans. "Right here."

"The girls are going to totally flip when they see this."

"No kidding."

Carla went to the rack of lifejackets and began twisting them on their hooks so the jackets' backs faced out. With a snap of her fingers, she signaled for Skyla to toss her a spray can.

"What're you going to put?" Skyla asked.

"Oh, the usual: tramp, whore, bi—"

A low rumble filled the shed.

The girls jumped.

"What was that?" Skyla whispered.

"Don't know," Carla said softly. She waited a moment. The sound didn't repeat itself.

"Think someone's outside?"

"Maybe . . ." She glanced back at her friend and smiled. "Nah. It's just us."

Carla shook the can of paint. No sooner did she write the letter W on one of the jackets did the rumble return. With a shriek, the girls jumped away from the lifejackets.

The double doors to the shed began to shake in their hinges, rattling in time with the rumbling.

Then silence. The shed was quiet again.

Carla tiptoed to the shed doors and peered through the crack between them.

"See anything?" Skyla asked.

"I'm looking."

Outside there was nothing but the empty area in front of the boat shed, the canoes sitting on their racks off to the side, just like they were when she and Skyla first entered.

Carla turned back to her friend. "There's nothing there."

Skyla hugged herself. "I think we should go. We can do this some other time."

But I want to do this now, Carla thought. "They hate us. You know it. I know it. We can get back at them and—"

If there was someone or something out there, she also realized they could not be caught in the shed fooling around.

The rumbling resumed and the doors banged, angling inward toward the girls, the hinges barely hanging on, the wooden latch outside sounding as if it would give way any moment. The girls screamed.

The doors banged, rattled, and shook violently as the girls heard footsteps crunching on the dirt outside. The footsteps passed by the doors and then by the walls, as if whoever it was seemed to be running in circles around the shed, faster than anyone was capable.

The girls backed further into the shed and hid behind the spare onboard motor sitting on a slat of wood about a foot off the ground.

The doors banged twice, then the shed was quiet once again.

"Ohmigosh, what's happening?" Skyla said, her teeth chattering, frightened.

"Don't know. Don't know. There's something out there and—"

"Do you think someone's screwing with us? You know, a joke?"

The thought had never occurred to her. Maybe it was a few of the girls, having seen them sneak into the shed, pulling a prank? Carla wouldn't put it past them.

Outside, the running footsteps circling the shed returned.

"I'll check," Carla whispered, then, calling out, "'Kay, guys. This isn't funny. Who's ever out there can quit it!"

The footsteps continued, now accompanied by a low tapping on the walls.

"I'm serious!" Carla stood up and Skyla followed her, marching over to the doors. "Guys, I mean it! Quit it or you're going to pay big time."

She squeezed her fingers through the crack in the door and fumbled with the latch outside. The moment her fingertips touched it, the rumbling resumed.

Skyla shrieked, sending a jolt up Carla's spine. Carla undid the latch and the doors opened.

There was no one outside.

Stepping cautiously out of the shed to check if anyone was hiding around the corner, Carla's neck and back muscles tensed when Skyla's shaky breathing suddenly grew quiet behind her. When she turned around, she shrieked.

Skyla was on the ground, writhing in pain, a red liquid-like creature on top of her.

What is that thi—Before Carla could finish her thought, the smooth surface of the creature's face peered up at her, and though it had no discernible features, it seemed to see right through her with eyes of fire.

Carla shrieked again and the thing returned to its work. Mesmerized, Carla watched as the creature began to cover Skyla's body in a red gel, her skin seeming to soak up the creature as though she was dirt in a plant's pot desperately needing water. The red goo slithered and slid all over Skyla, crawling under her white Camp Silverway T-shirt. The sloppy, sucking sound the thing made as it began joining itself with her only added to the hypnotic effect.

It took a moment before Carla realized she was just standing there, watching as this thing took her best friend. *Don't just stand there. Do something! It's . . . it's*—But what *was* it doing? Eating Skyla? Killing her? She didn't know. As she took a step toward the creature, she hoped it wouldn't notice. She didn't know what she was going to do or how she was going to get the thing off Skyla, but she had to do something, and fast.

"Hey!" she called out. The creature continued sucking on Skyla. "Hey! Get off her! Get—"

Suddenly, the creature slid back, withdrawing its goo-like hands and fingers from Skyla, and lunged at her. The moment the red goo touched her skin, Carla suddenly was filled with a comforting warmth, as though a damp quilt soaked in hot water covered her.

Regardless of a strange, pleasing sensation on her skin, she screamed and turned, her legs barely working beneath her as she ran toward the camp. The creature slid off her back. Glancing over her shoulder as she ran, she saw it just standing there as though the thing was indecisive as to whether to pursue her or continue feasting.

Skyla, no. Don't be dead. Don't be. Her body lay before the shed doors, unmoving. *I'm sorry.* Carla dug her heels into the ground, forcing herself to run away no matter how badly she wanted to see if her friend was all right.

She heard the creature's footfalls sounding like bare feet splashing through puddles as it decided to pursue her after all.

Come on. Run! You can do it. "Help! Someone, help! Is anyone out here?" The camp was deserted. *Where is everyone?*

She felt the heat of the creature behind her now, almost upon her, while up ahead, a man was running toward her, a black cape billowing behind him.

Chapter Five
The Ring Begins to Form

Aʙᴏᴜᴛ ᴛᴏ ʀᴜɴ into him, the man in the cape reached out, catching her by the arm.

"There! There!" Carla said, her voice laden with tears as she pointed in the direction of the creature speeding toward them.

With a sure hand, he guided her behind him. His black cape smelled of smoke, as though recently draped next to a bonfire.

The red creature dove into the air and in the time it took for Carla to acknowledge that the creature left the ground, the man raised a forearm covered with a silver gauntlet. There was a high-pitched mechanical sound, and the man's shoulder recoiled as a bright blue ball of flame spilled from the gauntlet's end, the flame wrapping itself around the creature like a large hand. The Bloodan fell to the ground with a splash and lay there in a pile of red goo.

"Go back to the others," the man said firmly.

Others? Who—Then Carla realized he meant for her to find the other girls in the camp.

She turned to run away but stopped in her tracks when she heard a growl coming from behind. Over her shoulder, she saw the creature regain its form and slide up into the air as though the air was a wall; the creature reformed itself into the shape of a man. The man in the cape darted toward it and with a blur of silver and the twirl of a cape, another bright burst of blue flame exploded in the gooey creature's middle. The red-man wailed as it flew backward in the air, exploding in a firework of bright red peppered with what appeared to be blood.

The man in the cape turned toward Carla. "One for warning. Two for glory." Then, after a pause, "Usually."

Carla didn't follow. If that was a joke, it was lost on her. She concentrated on the rushing of footsteps behind her and soon Mary was at her side, embracing her.

Carla broke down and cried into the counselor's shoulder, thinking of Skyla and the amazing friend lying motionless by the boat shed.

Several paces away, Tarek gazed at his reflection in the polished silver gauntlet; his blurred and distorted reflection stared back.

There were two of them, he thought. *Bloodans. But, two is better than two thousand. Better than three thousand. They just keep coming. I need to know how many more are out there. Mary said there were more. My, how many?*

Mary eyed him as she rubbed Carla's back, consoling her. Tarek hoped his gaze told her that, although he was going to leave her for now, he would be back should he be needed again. She seemed to understand and closed her eyes as Carla told her over and over again what happened to Skyla.

Leaving the two girls, Tarek observed the camp, searching for more red-men.

They're out there. They have to be. They wouldn't send just, what, two? Three? Wait. "Send" isn't the right word. The barrier has been broken. They leaked *through.* The evil within the Bloodans, the essence of the darkness that drove them . . . there had been too many of them. Their power had separated the Veil of Time and they emerged in a period far before their eventual surfacing on the Earth. *I wonder if there is a way to send them back?* He supposed there was. If there was a way for the Bloodans to journey to the past, there surely must be a way to send them back to the future. *But how?* He feared he might never have an answer.

Tarek walked along the forest's edge, where it met the campground. The muscles in his neck and shoulders ached, apprehensious, numbed with caution.

"Those bloody things better show themselves. I should have brought more men back with me, but there was no time to prepare. I can only do so much." Gazing along the grass, in the holes between the bushes and trees he walked by, he thought back to when, in a time yet to occur, he saw the Veil of Time tear in two and a Bloodan sneak through.

The muddy field was littered with the bodies of his fallen comrades in their struggle against the Bloodans. Smoke hung in the air like a tarp of gray with visibility less than three feet. All around, the black shadows of Bloodans silhouetted against the matte of gray, running about, the shadows of soldiers torn down the moment a Bloodan snuck near them. Tarek was the leader of his Pack, a group of a dozen or so men who worked as a team to take down the creatures. There were over one hundred Packs in his part of the world, with many more Packs elsewhere. The Bloodans *were* everywhere. If Tarek and those like him did not defeat the Bloodans, the race of Man would soon be overrun and these foul creatures would have control of the Earth. He knew, however, they would also eventually die. They needed humans and their blood to provide nourishment and strength.

That first Bloodan, the one that originally slipped through the Veil of Time, was the one who attacked

Cabin Seven that summer back in 1982. He supposed whenever a Bloodan first emerged in a place it did not know, it acted out of fear, relying on its instinct to kill to survive. He didn't know that the barrier separating one time period from another split until he emerged through the Veil in Camp Silverway those many years ago. He didn't know he had traveled in time, just that somehow, by following the Bloodan, he had been transported to elsewhere in the world. However, when he saw the night sky was a deep purple and not the dark red he was accustomed to, he realized he wasn't in *his* world at all. Fortunately, the slit in time remained open that night in '82 long enough for Tarek to return to his time once he killed the Bloodan and saved the cabin full of teenage girls.

Now, the Bloodans were back at Camp Silverway. What was it about this location that made it so special? If Tarek was correct in assuming that even though he was in a different time but his *location* was the same, then maybe it was due to all the bloodshed here, or bloodshed to come. Maybe, in his time period, the evil in the Bloodans caused openings in time to spring up sporadically and specifically in this one location.

There's really no way to know for sure, he thought. *To me, I left this place less than a day ago but here, everything's changed. I wonder if, between when I first came here and now, if more Bloodans surfaced, if more have killed. However, I suppose if they had, then maybe this place wouldn't be standing anymore. I'm lucky to have found Mary. I'm glad someone from before is here with me now. Loneliness is a terrible thing.*

Off to the left, there was movement in the trees. As he parted branches and stepped around small shrubs, he thought back to the last parting of the Veil of Time, the moment before standing in Camp Silverway.

The Bloodans had overrun his camp, killing most of his men. They covered nearly all of the bodies and sucked heavily on their veins, sinking into the men, drinking every last ounce of blood before the bodies would be of no use to them or, if they chose, they *merged* with them.

He had been fighting off as many as he could, but not quickly enough. Well over two-dozen Bloodans surrounded him, while he kept hoping his gauntlet would power up before they attacked.

Suddenly, a red dot faded into existence, surfacing in the smoke. It soon grew, forming a spinning disc twirling ever faster until it went upright and narrowed, splitting the air as though someone had carved through it with a knife. All the Bloodans ducked as the air and smoke came at them in a rush. Tarek remained standing, keeping his balance as the wind tried to knock him over. There, through the slit in the air, he saw the blue of an afternoon sky and the green of woods and logs of a building somewhere far off.

In a moment of confusion, the Bloodans screeched and one scrambled into the slit. It wasn't until Tarek was running after it and already part way through the Veil did he realize he was going back in Time *again*.

He was behind the Bloodan that got through and wasn't aware as to how many more followed. It was only when he emerged in Camp Silverway and he ran off into the trees after the Bloodan, did he stop and watch as the Veil began closing itself. His heart pounded at the idea of being trapped here. His men needed him; those still alive, anyway. Without him . . . . He needed to finish what they started. He couldn't leave the few left there alone. But the Bloodans . . . they were here, now, in Camp Silverway, as was he.

Now, wandering through the trees, searching for any more Bloodans that might have got through the Veil, he checked his gauntlet, making sure it was ready to be used at a moment's notice. The gauntlet hummed on his forearm, ready to spew forth another brilliant ball of blue flame if it had to.

He looked forward to using it again.

In the mess hall, Mary sat with Carla on her lap, rocking the girl back and forth, trying to calm her down. But despite the words of comfort, and soothing touches, she knew they weren't helping enough to make a difference.

Poor thing, Mary thought. *I know exactly what she's going through. I felt the same way when I saw that thing attack Becky. When I saw it hang on to Doug as though it needed him. When I saw it take Shelly. I still feel it now and it makes me sick to think I could have done something, anything, to help them. I don't think there's anything I can say to her that would make the pain go away, but I pray I can.*

Carla pulled her head away from Mary's shoulder, disbelief on her face, her eyes red and swollen, tears still pooling at their edges.

"I can't believe she's gone," she said.

Mary glanced to the window behind Carla, hoping to see Tarek walking by. But all she saw was the green of the forest's leaves and the brown of the cabins. "Neither can I."

"I-I've never . . . I've never lost anyone. Not right in front of me. The only person I knew who died was my grandpa, but he was in a hospital when it happened and I wasn't there." She wiped tear-soaked strands of brown hair away from her eyes and sniffled. "Is there—was there anyone you knew who . . . who . . ." She didn't finish.

"Yes," Mary said. The memory of Becky encompassed in that glob of red goo caused her heart to sink into her stomach. And Doug . . . that look of helplessness in his eyes when it happened, with a gaze that said he was surrendering to the thing. And Shelly, the first time she witnessed a Bloodan attack someone. "There were two who . . . that those things took." She wiped at the tears building in her eyes. Becky and Doug, friend and boyfr—There was another, too. "Actually," she continued, "Shelly survived thanks to that man you saw. So three. But what happened to Shelly was a long time ago. Becky . . . died and Doug—Doug was my friend" —*or was he my boyfriend? I loved him but we never really dated officially*— "I thought those things were gone. I was wrong and earlier they . . . they killed him." She put a hand over her face and wept.

Carla brought her in for a hug and the two welcomed each other's comforting touch. When their embrace loosened, Carla was the first to speak.

"I never saw anyone get killed before. Never. On TV, yeah, I've seen that. And in movies. But not in front of me. I don't think anyone should ever see that. Ever."

"What were you two doing out by the shed?" Mary asked. She saw a flicker in Carla's gray eyes.

"N-Nothing. Just playing . . . um, just playing hooky. We didn't want to go cl-climbing. Skyla is scared—was scared—of heights."

Mary gave her a sympathetic grin. *It's always hard to not think of the person as still around. "Is" to "was." That takes courage.*

"What do we do now?" Carla asked.

Mary ran a hand through Carla's silky brown hair. "I don't know. We should stay here though. Sarah's gone to get the others. She'll bring them all back here so they can wait for their parents to take them home."

"What about the school bus out back?"

It was an old rickety thing driven once a summer when the counselors took the girls into the small town nearby for ice cream and a movie.

"The guy who was supposed to come out and give it a once-over never showed. It's not running for some reason. We tried it. None of us knows how to fix the thing so we were going to do something else this year instead of a movie."

"Oh," Carla said, sounding disappointed. "I hope everyone gets back here soon."

Mary gazed at her own reflection in the polished oak table beside her. "Me, too."

Tarek emerged from the forest and immediately got down on one knee. By the polished leather of his boot, there was a dark band of red, about two feet in width, already six or seven inches high.

Blood.

It was beginning.

Tarek touched the blood. He rubbed the oily, red liquid between his fingers.

"The border's going up," he said to himself.

He glanced off to his right along the edge where the forest met the clearing. There was a dark line spanning along the edge and he knew it wasn't a shadow. The dark line stretched and followed the horseshoe form of the forest, like a wall around a castle.

The Bloodans were making their move.

There has to be at least fifty out here, if not more. Three or four Bloodans couldn't create that. He knew it wouldn't be long until that dark line grew.

He had to warn the others.

Chapter Six
Thou Shalt Not Leave

ALL THE CAMPERS gathered in the mess hall, sitting at the tables and huddling together as if they were all best friends. They had each called their parents for an early pickup, using the cover story that Camp Silverway was closing up early due to a harsh flu going around. Some of the other girls got extraordinarily "sick" and the counselors didn't want it to infect anyone else. It was a lie, but it was either that or tell their parents the truth about the Bloodans. They knew their parents wouldn't believe them that monsters had come and invaded the camp never mind the media frenzy that would ensue if they did. Mary didn't know if the creatures knew about the world beyond and she certainly wasn't going to be a part of informing them. Yet, with that border of blood around the camp—maybe the girls should meet their folks far on the other side of it to ensure its presence was kept a secret?

She sat with Carla and Sarah at the center table, along with Jenna, Lana and 'Nessa.

The girls talked quietly, their whispers creating a strange *buzzing* in the air, like the humming of bees that suddenly had their volume turned on low.

"I hope they don't take too long," Jenna said.

"Who?" Lana asked.

"My parents. We live about an hour away from here but knowing them, it'll take them two hours to get here. They always seem to take it easy, the whole 'we'll get there when we get there' thing, even when it comes to stuff that's important."

Lana turned to Mary. "What are we supposed to do until our folks get here?"

Pray, she wanted to say, but instead said, "We'll stay here indoors where it's safe. I don't want anyone going outside. We have all we need here. Your bags are all by the doors. And . . ." She eyed the girls; they looked back at her eagerly ". . . we got each other." *But is that enough? Maybe I should tell them that in a bit we'll take the bags and head past the camp entrance?*

Just then, Tarek was with them. Mary hadn't heard him approach. The room went suddenly quiet.

"They need to go," he told Mary. His voice was as cold as frostbite.

Mary felt stares upon her and how the girls' eyes shifted between her and Tarek. When she spoke, her voice was calm with resolve. "That's what they're doing. They're waiting here until their parents arrive."

"No."

No? Maybe he's thinking the same thing I am?

When Tarek's cool gaze settled upon her, she felt a chill run up her spine. "They leave now," he said. "Something's happening out there" —he nodded toward the window— "and it's best they go as soon as possible."

"But they can't leave. We have no way to take anyone anywhere. Our bus doesn't work and—"

"Bus?" He didn't seem to understand what a bus was. Before she could finish explaining their transportation dilemma, he turned away. He ran his hand along his gauntlet, stroking it gently. "The wall is going up," he said as he glanced back at her. "It's a tactic they use to keep everyone in. There is no escape. I can't even blast my way through it." He raised the gauntlet. "This is strong. It's one of the few things that can hurt them."

"Just that?"

"The fire. But it won't matter unless we leave. The Bloodans will keep us here."

"Is it special? I mean, is it just fire or is there something more to it?" *I've never seen fire that blue before.*

"It's regular fire, if there is such a thing. This" —he looked at the gauntlet— "creates flame, releasing only the hottest part, the blue part, the flame's base, for lack of a better word. It . . . it's hard to explain but, essentially, it extracts the blue from the flames it creates and combines them into what you see when it fires."

Sarah stood up and folded her arms, but not before brushing long strands of blonde hair out of her eyes. "How long do we have?"

"An hour, maybe less. Once the wall begins, it goes up quickly. Everyone needs to leave."

For some reason, Mary felt it was weird listening to Tarek talking to someone else other than her. "But how are we going to do that?" she said. "Leave, I mean. Like I said, there's no way out."

Tarek moved toward her. He was at least a foot taller than she. "Why don't you just walk? I don't know what this 'bus' thing is you're talking about, but you have legs—Use them!"

The campers erupted into an indistinguishable blur of murmuring. Then Mary heard one of the girls ask another if this guy was for real.

"So we're just supposed to walk to town?" Sarah said.

"Yes," Tarek said. "It's either that or we die."

You created panic. That wasn't wise, Tarek thought. He sat outside the lodge on the wooden steps that led up to the porch. He held his gauntlet out at the ready in case a Bloodan tried a surprise attack.

The door behind him opened and Mary sat down beside him. "We talked it over."

You shouldn't have talked it over. You should have just listened. "And?"

"We're leaving. Now."

"Good." He paused. Then, "I want to show you something."

Tarek stood and walked cautiously along the front of the lodge and rounded its right side, with Mary following close behind.

"See that?" he said, pointing off a ways ahead of him.

Mary's mouth fell open.

The red wall was as clear as day. It was about two and a half feet tall and two feet wide. It rippled and pooled like a stream, but there was nothing holding it in place. The liquid seemed to be made of gelatin, holding a life of its own. The wall rolled up and down along the forest's edge in an uneven wave, some parts taller than others, but he told her that soon, the wall would be one level, then eventually rise up on all sides until it covered the camp in a dome.

She said, "I can't believe it. It's . . ."

"I suggest you get them out right away. We can cross where the wall is low."

"But the forest?"

"We'll go in and walk until we find open land. This place isn't safe anymore. Go inside and tell the others. Either we do this now or we're all dead, I assure you." He looked her in the eye. "The Bloodans are everywhere."

A short time later, the girls were gathered outside with Mary, Sarah and Carla at the front. Tarek faced them.

"Everyone needs to stick together. If you do, we'll be fine. Don't stray. Hold hands if you have to," he said.

The girls talked amongst themselves.

They don't know if they can trust him, Mary thought. *I mean, look at him. He looks like something out of a history movie, and that thing on his forearm, that gauntlet . . . the girls know it's dangerous. The fire that thing spews—*

"Let's go," Tarek said, startling Mary from her thoughts.

They proceeded toward the forest. Mary's legs were shaky, and she knew Sarah's and Carla's could not be any better. The red ring forming along the forest's edge had grown by another foot since he told her to go into the mess hall and retrieve the others. They would still be able to step over it—just barely—but Tarek said that once the wall got going, it would keep growing faster and faster until they were trapped like lambs in a slaughterhouse.

As the girls approached the red wall, a loud shriek filled the air. Then another, and another. Three Bloodans sprang out of nowhere and pounced on three of the girls, swiftly taking them to the grass. There was the same disgusting sucking sound as they glommed onto the girls and started seeping into them.

More Bloodans appeared, over ten of them, by Mary's estimate, shrieking, diving into the group, and bringing the girls down.

"Go on. Go! Jump over the wall and get into the forest. Hurry!" Tarek shouted, waving his arms, encouraging the girls to listen.

Those left standing from the attack scrambled toward the wall. Two of the girls fainted after the first step when they saw the Bloodans feast upon their friends.

A flush of relief washed over Mary's heart when she heard the *powering-up* sound from Tarek's gauntlet.

Thank God, she thought. *Sarah* . . . "Sarah, help them! Get them out of here!"

"All right," she replied and tried her best to keep the girls calm as they rushed toward the wall.

The campers all screamed as a few jumped over it; one tripped, the red wall swallowing her foot whole, sucking her into it, carrying her off and under, down the stream of blood.

Mary ran over to Tarek, his arm already raised. Suddenly, his shoulder jerked back and a brilliant blue ball of flame shot forth from the gauntlet, tearing into one of the Bloodans coming toward them. As he waited a moment for his gauntlet to power up again, he turned to Mary. "Go!"

"No!" she said. *Did I just say that? What? Why?*

"I said go!" He gave her a shove in the direction of the red wall.

She put a hand on his shoulder. "What about you?"

"I'll be fine," he said. "Take the others and leave. It's my job to destroy them."

More of the girls fell as the Bloodans, once finished their drinking—absorbing—the blood of the others, jumped on them and wrestled them to the ground.

Sarah turned to Mary, her hand frantically waving. "Mary, let's go. Now!"

As Tarek fired off another ball of flame at a Bloodan running toward him, another Bloodan pounced on him from behind and took him down. Mary screamed, hands immediately covering her mouth.

The gauntlet powered up and he fired off another round. The creature flew back, landing five feet away in a splash. Tarek was quick to his feet.

As though happening in slow motion, Mary watched as the Bloodan gathered itself together, taking on its humanlike form. Slowly, Tarek's arm raised and the powering-up sound seemed to draw on for an eternity. The Bloodan leaped into the air, flying at a snail's pace toward Tarek. As though easing himself down, Tarek got on one knee and raised the gauntlet. Mary moved to the side, slowly.

Then time sped up again and as the creature was about to land on top of Tarek, another shot of fire blasted out of the gauntlet's end.

Suddenly, there was a low, swishing sound, like water moving around in a tub.

Oh no, Mary thought. The red wall rose, the blood creating it swirling like Kool-Aid in a pitcher. It spiraled upward quickly, gaining at least four feet, as a sudden rush of blood filled it further.

"It's growing rapidly now. Their feeding is making it grow," Tarek said. "Are the girls gone?"

A quick glance around the camp told Mary not everyone had gotten over the wall; Bloodans sucked on the girls' bodies, seeping into them.

Is it just me or have they— "—multiplied," she finished. At least a dozen more had appeared and one of them was rushing toward her, the others charging toward Sarah, Carla, and the girls, who could only stand before the wall and not go over since it was now too high and too thick in width.

Tarek fired off another round of blue flame, defending Mary as a Bloodan was almost upon her. The creature fell back and splooshed against the ground. Mary ran over to Sarah, trying to get away before it recreated itself and came at her again.

"We can't keep this up," Mary said.

"What do we do now?" Carla asked.

"We should get inside," Sarah said.

No kidding, Mary thought. "But how—"

The Bloodans, having finished feeding, began pulling themselves out of the girls' bodies, drawing themselves back and upwards, remolding into the featureless humanlike forms that sent shivers along Mary's skin. There were now too many and no way for them to run toward the lodge—to get *indoors*—without getting killed.

Mary's eyes watered at the sight of the girls' limp bodies lying lifeless on the ground in odd positions, their skin tainted red from the Bloodans' touch. They were so young, died without ever really having lived. Nevertheless, she knew it was better for them to die than live with the memory that was happening right before her eyes.

There was another heated blast of fire as Tarek managed to pick off two more Bloodans.

"We need to leave," he shouted. "You should have gone when you had the chance. Get indoors now! I can't hold them off much longer." He fired off another round.

The three girls jumped when a Bloodan fell before them, landing in a splash with blood spattering their shoes.

"How? There's so many?" Carla practically screamed at him. She hopped up and down, panicking.

"Wait—Move!" he said.

The girls ran toward him when they caught sight of a couple of Bloodans closing in on them; they hid behind Tarek as though he was a shield.

"There's too many," Sarah said.

"What are we going to do?" Mary asked him. Her insides were jelly, her stomach racked with fear. *Please, think of something.*

"I have an idea," Tarek said. He opened up a panel on the gauntlet's face, meddling with something within.

The four of them stepped back slowly, following Tarek's lead. Mary glanced over her shoulder and saw Bloodans behind them. Tarek was still fiddling with something in his gauntlet.

"If you're going to do something, do it quick," Mary said.

"Just wait," he said, his voice calm, as though he had done this countless times before.

The two Bloodans coming toward them moved in graceful steps, as though gliding along the grass rather than stepping on it, and the ones behind them moved with the same fluidity. The creature that had fallen and splashed on the girls' toes was already reforming itself and sliding toward them.

Tarek spoke. "When I count to three, crouch down."

"What?" Sarah asked.

"Crouch down. On three. One, two—" The Bloodans flew up in the air, arms out, jelly-like fingers outstretched, ready to grab. "Three!"

The four of them crouched down, Sarah and Carla screaming, Tarek releasing a battle cry, Mary the only one silent.

From the pointed tip of Tarek's gauntlet, a blue wave of fire blew forth, at least eight feet wide and one foot thick, slicing into the Bloodans midair, toppling them over like a person hit in the gut with a baseball bat. Before the three liquid bodies began to fall, Tarek spun the blue wave of fire around and nailed more that avoided the blast and moved to attack from behind.

Crap, that's hot! Mary thought as the wave of blue fire blew over her. Tarek, crouched down as well, faced her, his grim face washed in the glow of bright blue, sweat glistening off his cheeks.

The Bloodans screeched as the fire split them in two and they fell to the ground.

"Let's go. Run!" Tarek was already on his feet, pulling Mary behind him, Sarah and Carla desperately trying to keep up.

"What are we doing?" Sarah asked the same time Carla said, "Where are we going?"

Tarek didn't answer, instead leading them back to the lodge, weaving around the creatures coming toward them as they tried to make it to safety.

Chapter Seven
Indoors

THE DOORS IN the main foyer and the exit that ran off the kitchen were secured by stacking tables against them. To add weight to the tables, Mary, Sarah, Carla and Tarek put drawers of cutlery and other kitchen tools on them, along with the books that lined the mess hall walls a few feet shy of the ceiling. Mary had to stand on the last remaining table to reach them.

"What about the windows?" Sarah asked from across the room. She was by the window with Carla.

"We have nothing to brace them with," Mary said. "We could use the cupboard doors from the kitchen, but we have no way of taking them off then putting them on the windows. All the tools are in the maintenance shed." She pulled the last of the books off the bookshelf and climbed down off the table. She dumped them on to the stack of books already on a table by the door, and then came back into the eating area.

Carla, her arms crossed, gazed out the window at the dead bodies littering the field, and at the Bloodans attached to a few of the girls, still feeding, still seeping into them. Sarah stood beside her, leaning against the windowpane.

Mary went over to Tarek, who was sitting on the ground, cross-legged, his gauntlet on his lap. When he looked up at her, defeat was in his blue eyes.

"It took too much out of it. Far too much," he said. He glanced down at his gauntlet. "It was the only way to save us. Now there's nothing I can do. I melted the firing mechanism. I'm not sure how I'm going to replace it."

"Who built those things?" Mary asked.

"A fellow by the name of Will Baron. But that was a long time ago" —he smirked— "or will be in a short while or . . . . I don't know. Regardless, I didn't build it. My men and I were given these while training to be part of the struggle against the Bloodans. Because time was short, we didn't have the chance to learn the details of how they worked. We were needed in the field right away. We were only taught the basics, enough to manipulate them should the need arise. But . . . fighting day and night, there's no time for anything else. If you're not fighting, you're resting. No time even for learning." He withdrew his hand from the inner part of the gauntlet and rested it on his knee. "It's no use."

"Keep trying."

A questioning expression filled his face along with a stern gaze.

"I mean, can you keep trying? We have to do something."

"I know." Tarek got to work.

Outside, the red wall grew thicker, having become a dome over Camp Silverway, holding captive all inside.

It was early evening and the darkening sky was visible through the blood-red transparence of the dome. The creatures left the girls' bodies on the field, the bodies drained, the girls' skin pale in places, red-blotched in others, empty and shrunken to their skeletons like mummies in museums.

There was no wind; the elements outside the dome had no influence on the camp within. And if that was true, air was limited.

The Bloodans were gone from around the lodge.

For now.

The four ate canned beans and fruit cups for dinner and drank tall glasses of milk. They sat around the table Mary had used as a stepping-stool to grab the last of the books off the shelf. They ate mostly in silence, an uneasiness settling between them.

"We can't just stay here," Carla said. After the room being quiet for so long, her voice was uncomfortably loud.

"Right now this is the safest place for us," Tarek said.

"But we're going to have to get out sooner or later. Who knows how long those things will be out there."

Tarek chewed slowly on a slice of peach from his fruit cup. "They'll stay out there, waiting for us. They won't go. Not with us in here."

"Then what should we do?" Sarah asked.

"We have to get past that wall," Mary said, tapping her fork against the side of her can.

"How?" Carla said.

"I have no idea. Tarek?"

He set his fork down and leaned back in his chair. "Let me think a moment. There's always a way. We just have to find it."

His words were not encouraging.

How do you find a way out through a wall of red goo that sucks you in the moment you touch it? Mary thought back to the girl that was carried away by the wall's red current when they first tried to escape. She was ashamed she couldn't remember the girl's name.

"Do you think they'll come in here?" Sarah asked Tarek.

"Eventually," he said. He leaned forward and put his elbows on the table, palms flat. "They're like children. Though vicious, this is all just a game to them. We hide, they find us, they confront us, we run. But, like all children, they grow weary of the game they're playing and bring it to an end."

Mary shivered.

"You didn't really answer the question," Carla said. "Will they get in here?"

"Yes. Once the game is over."

"So we're coaxing them to play," Sarah said.

Mary drifted off into her memories as images from the night in '82 came back to her. She could still smell the wooden panels of Cabin Seven, still hear the screams of the girls as the Bloodan began seeping its way into Shelly. The awful sloshing, slurping sound it made as it dug itself deeper and deeper into the helpless girl. In her mind, she was now back on that top bunk, looking down and seeing Shelly struggle through a haze of red liquid. There was the cracking of wood, a loud snap. Wood splintering, and Tarek standing in the doorway, a bright blue flame flying forth from the gauntlet on his forearm. She could see him through the gaps between her fingers, just beyond the strands of brown hair that hung over her eyes. In her recollection, Tarek looked at her, looked *through* her. She hadn't noticed before, but it seemed he was confident they would meet again.

"Mary?" His voice was strong, like that of a father's. "Mary?"

She was back in the mess hall, Tarek across from her, Sarah and Carla on either side.

"Sorry," she said, "just thinking." *I need out.*

"Sarah just suggested we try the two-way in the bus," Carla said.

Two-way? Wh—Then she understood. "But how do we get out there? If those things come, we have no way to defend ourselves." She eyed Tarek's gauntlet, the pointed end of it now melted.

"Fire," Tarek said.

"What?" Sarah asked.

"Fire. Blue flame."

Mary stood and put her hands on her hips. "But that weapon of yours is useless. It's not like we can fend them off with chair legs, forks and knives."

"Forks?—I have an idea. Never tried it before but it might work. Not as effectively as this" —he ran a hand over the gleaming silver finish of the gauntlet— "but it could buy us some time, help us get to this 'bus' safely enough. What's a two-way?"

"You don't know what a two-way radio is?" Carla immediately blurted out.

Tarek's cold stare told everyone at the table he didn't like being made fun of.

Carla slumped down in her chair, looking like a turtle ducking into its shell.

Sarah spoke up. "A two-way radio allows us to talk over large distances. Like a telephone." By the way he looked at her, it seemed Tarek didn't know what a telephone was either. "We might be able to contact someone who can help us."

"It's going to take more than one person to help us, my dear," he said, standing from the table and going over to the window. He wrapped his black cape around him like a blanket.

When it seemed Tarek was out of earshot, Carla whispered, "What?" to the other girls. Sarah just rolled her eyes.

"He's not from here," Mary said. "He's from—the future, or he says he is. Anyway, I believe him."

"You believe him." It was more of a statement.

"Yes." *Do I?* "It's the only way to explain those, those Bloodans." She placed her hands on the table, feeling the sweat on her palms make her skin slip on its smooth finish. "Tarek." He turned. "If we reach someone, they'll bring help. The world will see the dome. The Bloodans might escape."

"You are right, but perhaps humanity at this time has the means to put an end to the Bloodan threat before they take over everything."

"Maybe," she said. "What do you have in mind?"

The man in the cape only grinned.

Chapter Eight
Escape to the Bus

TAREK TOLD THE girls to wait indoors while he checked things outside. On the porch, there was no breeze, there was no temperature. It was neither hot nor cool. It was just air, stillness, and silence. The red liquid dome covering Camp Silverway isolated the camp from the rest of the world, the inside of this bubble a world of its own. He could tell the sky overhead, past the dome, was dark. It must be just past the nineteenth hour, if not the twentieth. He was surprised it took this long for it to be dark. Where he came from, the sun was hidden behind smoke and red by the eleventh hour.

The sky—the dome—was a deep red, bloodlike, rippling as though some otherworldly force was blowing on its surface from the outside. What made him uncomfortable was how the *rippling* didn't make a sound.

He carefully scanned the open ground before him, checking for Bloodans. The bus wasn't too far from here, just on the other side of the lodge, according to Mary.

He cautiously walked to the right and paused before looking around the corner. He had the gauntlet on his forearm, hoping the creatures wouldn't know it no longer worked. He peered around the corner. Nothing. Just the red tint of the dome on the trees, the grass and the dirt a browny shade of red. He paused a moment when his eyes settled on the lake. The red wall ran out about twenty feet into the water, cutting across the dock as it began to round back in.

I wonder— It was possible the barrier didn't extend all the way down to the lake's floor. *Let's try this two-way first.*

Mary thinks it might help. If it does work and we notify someone of our whereabouts, then *we can try the lake. We can also try it if this "two-way" doesn't save us. Two ways of what, I don't know. It's a dumb name.*

He kept his back to the wall as he turned the corner, listening for any movement, his eyes sharply focused on his surroundings. Back home, smoke, red mist and watery eyes blurred everything. Out here, he could swear he saw everything all at once.

As he approached the end of the wall, the only sound was his boots moving along the wooden planks of the porch. When he peered around the corner to the back of the property where the bus was, he was relieved when he saw there wasn't anything around that funny-looking yellow thing. All was clear.

He barely heard what sounded like two Bloodans sneaking up on him on the other side of the porch's railing.

Tarek hadn't come back. *Where is he?* Mary wondered. She went to the window overlooking the side porch and then to the window that looked out into the back. The bus stood there, partly surrounded by stout bushes and tufts of grass that had grown up and around the wheels after being neglected all spring and summer.

"See him?" Carla asked, coming up behind her.

She shook her head.

"Where did he go?" Carla began to sob. It seemed to Mary she couldn't help it, so she put her arms around her, trying to comfort her.

"I want to go home," Carla said. "And I miss Skyla. And that guy left us. He's one of them! He left us to die. We're going to die. You're going to die, Mary. Sarah and me, too. I'm going to die."

"Shhh," Mary soothed, "it'll be over soon. You're not going to die. No one is." She wished she could make herself believe that.

Sarah came over to them and the three girls held each other.

Over a half-hour passed and Tarek still hadn't returned. The three girls, led by Mary, stepped out onto the porch, each carrying a makeshift torch made from chair legs. The ends of the legs were wrapped in tea towels soaked in cooking oil from the kitchen and lit by the stove.

He told them it was the blue of the flame—the hottest part—that did the most damage. Yes, the yellow of the flame did harm them, but not nearly as much as the blue. Mary had a sudden flashback to Catholic School and hearing about the fiery lake of Hell. Could it be that's where these creatures were from and why fire could hurt them? She wasn't sure and didn't really care if she knew the answer or not. She just didn't want to be attacked again.

The girls moved along the porch like a group of cats sneaking along the lower wall of a fence ready to pounce on a squirrel or mouse, their eyes sharp, ready for anything.

Almost there, almost around to the back, Mary thought. *Where's Tarek? I hope he's not dead.*

Her heart seemed to rise in her chest, its pulse throbbing in her collarbone and throat. She could tell Sarah and Carla were also nervous and frightened by the sound of their short and shallow breathing.

The bus was around the corner, completely alone in the back of the property, off to the side by the bushes. It wouldn't take long to reach it, maybe only thirty-five, forty long paces; a fifteen-or-so-second run.

"Do you see him?" Carla asked.

"No," Mary said.

Groaning, Carla wiped a few tears from her eyes, evidently on the verge of falling apart.

Sarah put a hand to Carla's back and turned to Mary. "When do you want to do this?"

"The sooner the better," she said. She did not want to run out into the open to get to the bus. *I hope the door opens.* For some reason she thought it wouldn't. *No, don't think like that. Keep positive.*

"Like?" Sarah was waiting for more of an answer.

"On three," Mary said. "We run. Don't look around. Just go, up and over the railing. Once we're inside the bus—"

The two girls huddled up next to her. Sarah nearly pushed her over from the eagerness to get it done with.

"Okay, ready?" Mary whispered.

The other two nodded and the three of them silently counted it off, mouthing the numbers.

They ran.

Mary didn't slow when she approached the porch railing, instead planting her left hand firmly on the top plank, torch held up high in her right hand for clearance and, hopping on her toes, swinging her legs up and over. The ground was only five feet below her and there was a brief pause when she landed, bending at the knees to absorb the blow, before running again. Because of the change of wind from her speed, the heat from the torch's flame licked her nose. She winced and held the torch further away from her. She didn't look back to see if the other two got over the railing all right. *Why should I? I don't want to die. If we slow down—* A flush of relief washed over her when she caught Carla and Sarah in her peripheral. *Thank God.*

The air whistled by her ears as she ran, the flame of the torch she carried fluttering loudly. It wasn't until she was about ten feet from the bus did she notice the dark red sky above her. She stopped dead in her tracks and gazed upward through the semi-clear rippling ceiling of the blood dome into the late evening sky beyond. Sarah stopped beside her while Carla ran straight for the bus.

"Come on," Carla called with a wave of her hand. "Let's go!"

"I didn't realize how . . ." Sarah seemed to be at a loss for words at the sight of the red sky.

"Yeah, I know," Mary said.

For the briefest of moments she forgot where she was, forgot the Bloodans that might be circling the camp out of sight. She forgot so many had died. Forgot what they were supposed to be doing: getting to the bus.

A low rumble and the light, wet *fut-fut-fut* of footsteps brought her back to the here and now.

Bloodans.

"Go!" Mary shouted at Sarah. They darted for the bus.

Carla was at the big yellow folding doors, her fingers in between the crack, trying to pry it open. "It's stuck," she said, already panicking when the two girls caught up to her.

"Here," Sarah said as she moved her aside. She placed a palm on the long, rectangular window on the left, higher up on the door. She pushed, putting the most pressure where the door met the hinge. The door opened.

The *fut-fut-fut* grew louder, closer. Bloodans sprang forth from the trees, their bodies almost blending into the dark red tint over everything.

"Get in! Get in!" Carla pushed Sarah and Mary into the bus.

Mary plopped herself into the driver's seat and gripped the door lever, closing the door the moment the girls were in and a Bloodan rushed up.

Chapter Nine
Girls Awake

THE BLOODAN HIT the door in a red splash, splattering over the door's windows so thick Mary couldn't see outside. Through the windshield, Mary watched as more deadly creatures poured out of the bushes and leaped onto the hood. Some stayed there while others jumped past their kin and onto the roof. The bus rocked and the girls squealed with each tip to the side.

"Don't drop the torches!" Mary shouted.

There was no ventilation inside the bus and the air was stale. Mary didn't know how long they could last in there with the torches burning and not get smoked out. The bus kept rocking.

"We should just let them come in here, one by one," Carla said. "We can stand by the door and stick the torches into them, one at a time. I want to make them pay for killing Skyla."

For an instant, Mary entertained the idea. Then she realized the moment the doors opened, the creatures would overrun whoever was standing there and kill all three of them before they had a chance to escape. Besides, if they did come in one at a time, the torch's yellow flame might not hold up completely to their wet bodies.

"No," Mary said.

"I don't want those things coming in," Sarah said.

"But—" Carla screeched when one of them slapped its gel-like hands hard against the back door of the bus.

We have to do something, Mary thought. *The two-way!* She had nearly forgotten all about it. She snatched it up and as she turned on the squawk box, she told the other two girls to double-check the bus's windows and make sure they were closed along with the ventilation hatches on either end of the bus. Everything had to be secure, at least, for now.

Mary had never used a two-way before but she had seen it a million times in the movies. The box was small and black and had a couple of orange lights and gauges on it. She didn't know what they meant, but she slowly turned the channel dial and tried to find a signal without static. She prayed someone—anyone—would hear her.

In the background, Sarah yelped. There was a wet *thunk* against the side of the bus.

Each channel she tried was filled with static. Determined, she tried talking anyway, suppressing the button on the handheld mike and speaking into it loud and clear. "Someone help us! We're at Camp Silverway. Please answer. We need help!" She tried several more static-filled channels, each time with no answer. *Why won't this thing work?* She considered the red sky outside might have something to do with it. Who knew precisely *what* that dome was made of. It couldn't be *just* blood.

Sarah and Carla were back at the front of the bus.

"Everything's closed," Sarah said.

Carla came closer to Mary. "Is it working?"

"No," she said. "It's not." *It's not.*

Just then, all hope seemed lost.

Thunk.
Thunk.
Thunk.

The metal of the bus's hull pulsed low and dull. The Bloodans were gone from the windows. Whatever was making that noise was below view. This was the first time the sound returned in a good long while. None of the girls had the guts to go to the window and see what it was.

Thunk.

Thunk.

It was getting dark. Mary checked her watch and it was past ten. They'd been in the bus for over two hours, maybe more. Sarah's and Carla's stomachs growled; dinner hadn't been enough. Mary couldn't understand how they could be hungry. Her stomach was in knots.

The torches' flames burned only a few inches from their hands, the chair legs almost burnt to stubs. Thank God oak was slow-burning.

Thunk.

"It's them," Sarah said. "Those red people."

You think? Mary thought sarcastically. *'Kay, dumb thought.*

Carla shivered and briskly rubbed her bare arms. It was cooling off inside the bus. Mary wondered if it was cold outside as well and if that stillness on the air from before, that *absence* of weather because of the dome, had lifted. She thought also of Tarek. *He can't be dead. We need him.*

Time went on.

Sarah sat in the seat right behind Mary, who was still sitting in the driver's spot. Carla sat in the seat across from Sarah, her feet in the aisle.

Thunk.

Thunk.

*Thu—*Then a long scratching sound, like someone rubbing a sheet of sandpaper along the bus's metal side.

Sarah jumped and moved quickly to the edge of her seat, her feet in the aisle like Carla. She peered over her shoulder, glancing out the window.

"We can't stay here," Sarah said.

Mary agreed. They couldn't stay here, not inside an old bus with those things outside.

Thunk.

Another scrape and one last *thunk* before all grew still.

The girls sat motionless, anticipating the next low thud against the bus's exterior. None came.

Without realizing she was doing it until she was actually *doing* it, Mary cautiously approached the bus's door. She went down the two steps leading to it and stood in the doorway, the door still closed.

"Mary, don't," Sarah said.

She slowly leaned forward until her forehead rested on the glass, and peered outside. Camp Silverway was empty and dark. The sky appeared an even darker red, even more bloody. She put her fingers to the glass.

A face appeared in the window.

It was a girl—at least, at first glance, that's what Mary thought it was—one of the girls who fell victim to one of the Bloodans earlier. The form was female, curved and filled out in the hips and breasts. It was red and liquidy. Even the long *hair* atop its head was in red gel-like strands that hung over its smooth shoulders. It had no face but a confused gaze seemed to be there all the same.

Carla screeched. Mary took a step back, stumbling over the small, black step behind her. She landed on her bottom hard and she stayed there too terrified to move. She didn't want to provoke the red-girl outside. Didn't want to make it come in.

"Who's that?" Sarah asked, helping Mary back to her feet, slowly, carefully.

"I don't know. Can't tell. She's—she's one of them." Her legs wobbled beneath her once she stood.

"Whatdowedowhatdowedo." Carla's words slurred together and tears rolled down her cheeks.

Mary thought Carla's mind was going to collapse at any moment.

"Nononononononono . . ." Carla's teeth chattered loud enough for Mary to hear. "We have to go, need to leave, have to go, want out, please, Mary, please, get us out, try the radio, we must go, have to, have to, have to."

"Quiet. Just let me think," Mary said. Trying the radio again sounded good. Hope began to flow back into her. The torches . . . *If that thing comes in here, we'll use what is left of them and get it . . . her.*

There was another sandpaper-like scraping along the back of the bus. All three girls' heads turned in its direction, following the sound until another red female form appeared at the back door, hands against the window, the creature seeming to glance around as if she didn't understand the concept of a vehicle.

Thunk.

Thunk.

More girls, at least six of them. This time the tops of their red, liquid heads were seen along the bottom of the window frames, the jelly strands of "hair" sitting like noodles on their heads.

Thunk. Thunk. Thunk. Thunk. Thunk. Thunk.

THUNK. THUNK. THUNK. THUNK. THUNK. THUNK.

Thunk. Thunk. Thunk. Thunk. Thunk. Thunk.

The bus was surrounded.

"The torches," Sarah said. She held hers high, as though holding a sword. "We can open the top part of the windows and hit them with it." The blue part of the flame danced beneath the yellow teardrop wave above it.

Before they could agree on what to do next, the bus began rocking back and forth from the blood-girls outside pounding their hands against the bus. Mary felt the vibrations from their drumming in her chest, causing her to drop her torch and scramble to pick it back up. The bus shook again and she lost her balance, her hand landing on the flame. She yelped and cradled her palm. Thankfully, it was only a slight burn.

The window to the back door smashed open.

A girl—a *Bloodan*—crawled inside.

The side windows to the bus blew open in a spray of glass and the Bloodans slithered up the side of the bus, over the window frame and onto the dark leather seats like snakes.

Sarah was the first to move. She drove her torch into the Bloodan nearest her. The creature squealed but didn't back down. Carla plowed her torch into a Bloodan beside her, but to no effect.

Mary gathered enough courage to join them, and as the Bloodans neared, they tried to drive the creatures away, one at a time, stabbing them with their torches, even after the flames went out.

The bus kept rocking as more appeared outside. More scraping. More—*Thunk. Thunk. Thunk.*

Carla was the first to drop her torch. The moment the stub of the charred chair leg hit the bus's floor, the glass of the front door shattered and the first female Bloodan that approached the bus began to enter through its frame.

Rocking.

Thunk. Thunk. Thunk.

Scraping.

The girls were surrounded as the Bloodans pressed in, a look of hunger in their liquid, red faces.

Chapter Ten
An Unusual Creature

THE FEMALE BLOODAN gave Carla a twisted glare, as the bus rocked side to side. All three girls exchanged looks that said they thought the bus was going to flip over.

The bus tipped, the bus rocked, the bus teetered and—

It righted itself. The Bloodans within backed away, and then left the bus completely. The red faces in the windows sunk below view and disappeared.

"Where'd they go?" Sarah asked.

Mary swallowed the lump in her throat and saw a glimmer of red running by, then a matte of blood smeared all over the bus's rear door. The three of them looked on in terror as the creatures outside pressed against the back.

The bus lurched forward about a foot then slid back to where it was.

The Bloodans pressed again, fighting the brake pads holding the bus in park, and the bus jumped forward again. The girls lost their balance and nearly fell out of their seats.

The bus moved back and forth, front and back.

Once again it moved forward, and this time, didn't slide back. Branches snapped and leaves crushed as the yellow machine was pushed by the Bloodans, heading to who knew where.

What's going on? Where are they taking us? Mary thought. "Hold on to something," she said.

The two girls grabbed the backrests of the seats in front of them, and Mary hung onto the steering wheel. The creatures forced the bus forward, moving it past the lodge toward the lake.

They're going to dump us in!

The bus picked up momentum and began speeding toward the lake, bumping up and down as it traveled over the uneven ground. The dock came into view and . . . something else—another Bloodan, at least one and a half times the size of the others.

The creature stood at the edge, where the dock met the water. The bus continued toward it, picking up speed as it rolled. The moment the bus hit the dock, it shook with the vibration of the tires riding over the little gaps in between the planks.

Carla chattered along with it. "Du-du-du-du-du-duh."

Mary thought of the broken door to her right. *We could jump through. We'd get cut but we can jump through. We can do it.* Just as she was about to tell the other girls her idea, her eyes were drawn to the larger Bloodan at the end of the dock. It stood there, arms at its sides. It didn't look as *liquidy* as the other creatures. Its color was duller, more *powdery,* and more opaque. This Bloodan was different. Still red and liquid-like, but somehow different.

"Out the door! Jump!" Mary called to the others. She was already moving toward the door when the bus suddenly stopped as if hitting a deep rut. She slammed into the bar that bordered the front windshield, bruising her ribs and hip.

The two girls shot forward in their seats as well, while behind them, their tormenters shrieked and scraped the sides of the bus as they progressed toward the front of the vehicle. Mary backed up against Sarah and Carla and the three of them crowded into one of the seats in the middle of the bus, far enough away from the front and a safe distance from the back.

The big Bloodan, the one that was different, had its hands on the hood.

It had stopped the bus.

The other Bloodans crowded around it and the fight began.

Through red, hazy vision, Tarek watched his palms lift from the yellow—orange—of the bus's hood. He wanted so badly to jump onto the hood and fly through the windshield and seep himself into Mary, and then after her, the other two. *Oh, how good it would feel to sink into her, to flow with her blood, to circulate through her system, linger in her heart, rush out and slide around in her body,* he thought. *To feel her life. To feel their lives. To be them, one with them, separate yet together. Oh, please, let me do it. It would feel so good. It would—*

Quiet! Tarek ordered his feelings. His liquid form tingled with the need to indulge in the simple desire to drink, to eat, to absorb. *No! You are not one of them. Stop it. Stop it. Stop it! Leave them be. Let them g—*

The other Bloodans surrounded him. He knew what they wanted. They wanted to know why he stopped the bus from going over the edge of the dock. Once the bus was submerged in the water, the girls would put up less of a struggle, if any at all, too busy panicking to put up a fight. The water would open up the girls' pores even more and make the merging even easier, even sweeter. If Bloodans survived water, that was. *He* wasn't sure, but the change in his body instinctively told him it would work.

The Bloodans took a step forward and two of them leaped onto Tarek. His liquid arms collided with their bodies, for a moment intermingling together, before he pulled his arms away. When he touched them he could feel their malice, their distaste for humankind and what he was: half Bloodan, half Human.

For years, in his own era, he had been fighting them, watching them as they took over the planet, driving mankind into caves and holes in the ground. How he hated them. How he despised them. That rage, that luscious stream of pure anger, was his only tool. Now he was one of them. He experienced the merging when they took him away from the girls. He knew what it was like to have one of those foul creatures invade his body, bleed into his mind, try to control him.

But he was too angry to be controlled. Too pissed off to be manipulated into a mindless, blood-needing beast.

He could turn the tables on them. Switch things around. He was a part of their world now. But—

Another Bloodan grabbed him, mixed with him, and tossed him to the dock's planks.

Need to know how they do that, how they touch me, he thought. *Have to beat them. Grab onto them somehow.*

Another one pounced on him, pinning him to the dock, and started its merging, losing itself in him. He felt his liquid body interlocking with the creature's. *Have to use this to my advantage. Have to. Have to. Have to.* He pictured his liquid flesh. He pictured the creature's liquid flesh. He saw in his mind the red molecules joining, some of the creature's replacing his, some of his replacing the creature's.

He squeezed his insides—what he perceived as his molecules, his very composition, where the thing locked onto him. He gripped and felt his hold on the other's body tighten, then with a violent twist, he jerked onto his side, hurling the Bloodan free from himself, and over into the water. The two liquid bodies—the creature and the water—collided in a silent splash, which was more like a swallowing. Now he knew they had *two* weaknesses: blue fire and water. Maybe they didn't want to dump the girls over the edge after all.

Then it's safe to say, if the dome is made of the same thing as the Bloodans, that it does not reach down to the lake's floor. No wonder it never rains at home. They've taken over everything . . . even the weather. Everything's dried up and . . . His instincts earlier had been wrong. It had only been wishful thinking.

In their swirling red gazes, Tarek saw confusion setting in. *They're surprised I caught on.* The hunger hit him again. Mary. Sarah. Carla. Blood. Need it. Have to have it. Drink. Eat. Soak. Become one with them. *No!* The thoughts and feelings ravaged through him. He needed to feed. He wasn't thirsty yet his . . . soul? . . . yearned to be filled.

More Bloodans piled on him. In the background, somewhere past the mass of red bodies swarming over him, he heard the muffled screams of the girls inside the bus.

He had to get to them.

"I don't know why that thing stopped the bus and I don't care," Mary said. "They're all busy killing that . . . that big one. Let's go. Out the back. Come on. Move!"

Shoving Sarah aside, she ran down the aisle toward the back door with the others right behind.

Mary turned the handle and opened the rear door. The cracked glass from its window rattled in what was left of the frame as it flung open on its hinges, the door swinging open. She pushed it all the way open and hopped down onto the dock. Carla checked over her shoulder for any Bloodans that might be following them through the bus. There were none. Sarah jumped off the back of the bus first, Carla next. Once on the dock, the three ran for shore.

The moment Mary's foot touched land, the bus creaked and thumped as the Bloodans, still fighting the large one as well as still in contact with the bus, rocked it back and forth. Then, in an explosion of power, the bus flew up into the air, spun around and landed in the water a good fifteen feet from the dock. Carla screeched when the mass of Bloodans began slithering toward them like a giant snake, seeming to float above the dock's planks. The big Bloodan the creatures teamed up against lay in a heap at the far end of the dock.

There was no hope for escape.

Chapter Eleven
How Many Have to Die?

CARLA SCREAMED AGAIN. Sarah told her to be quiet and to start running. But she stood there, frozen. The staunch look of terror on her face told Mary she wasn't capable of moving.

"Carla, come on," Sarah shouted as she moved toward her.

Mary caught her by the arm. "No, stay here," she said. "Carla!"

But Carla still stood there, and the red tidal wave took her down. The giant blood-snake dove into her like a hurricane into a funnel, sucking, slurping, and soaking its way into her. Sarah screamed, tears rolling down her cheeks. Tears ran down Mary's face as well. She gave Sarah's arm another pull and urged her to run back toward the camp.

At the end of the dock, the big Bloodan got to its feet and took shaky steps to where the other creatures were merging with Carla.

Mary took one last look at the large Bloodan and for a brief moment, swore she saw it smile at her.

Tarek shuffled toward the others, surprised that he wasn't dead. *Can't kill what is already lost, can you?* He supposed not. His stomach—what he thought was his stomach—twisted in disgust as he watched the Bloodans, one by one, withdraw from Carla, leaving only a blood-soaked corpse near the edge of the dock. *She'll be with us shortly. She'll rise, changed, and feed with the rest of us. She'll return from the dead soon and—What am I thinking? What am I feeling? No more. I'm not one of them! I'm not!* But he was, he knew. He just would not let himself accept it.

The Bloodans, now a few feet away from Carla's body, set their red stares back onto him. He wasn't sure but thought he counted at least two dozen creatures, if not more. Too many. Too many for one man—creature—to handle.

The Bloodans moved as one toward him. Despite his better judgment, he welcomed their attack.

Time to die.

When they finally reached the lodge, Mary and Sarah were out of breath.

"Carla. Did you see? Did you see, Mary? She . . . she . . . she . . ." Sarah didn't finish.

"I know," Mary said. "They took her and . . ." She couldn't seem to finish her sentence either.

Mary took a quick glance toward the dock. No Bloodans were coming toward them. The dark red sky overhead swished and sloshed like a lake moving under a strong wind. But the waves high above didn't make a sound. And, strangely enough, Mary was already used to the sight of the red sky. It seemed to have always been there. That *red* had stuck with her all these years. That *red* that had glommed itself onto Shelly. That *red* that had blanketed her dreams, always seeming to surface in her mind when she saw a rose, or cherries at the supermarket, or the red Dodge Viper her neighbor owned.

"We're going to die here, aren't we?" Sarah said, sobbing.

Mary took her into her arms.

"I don't want to think about that but . . . yes, I think we will. There's no way out." Her heart hurt hearing herself say those words.

"I don't want to die. Please, Mary. You know I don't want to." Sarah was begging her, as if she had any control over what was going on.

"I don't either."

"But we will. Carla, Skyla, Becky, the girls . . . dead. All of them. We're next. I can feel it."

"Shhh, don't say that." She rubbed Sarah's back. "We'll get through this."

"But you just said there was no way out. How can we live if there's no way out?"

I don't know, she thought before saying it aloud. "I just wish I knew."

They had to get indoors. The sky was dark with the blood dome overhead, and their battle for survival was far from over.

Rage.

Uncontrollable.

Yet . . . manageable?

There was really no way to tell. One moment Tarek felt as if he was himself, a man who had seen more death and bloodshed in his life than any man should. The next, he was one of *them.* A creature without mind, driven only by need. It was as though he was upon a stone wall, humanity on one side, Bloodan on the other. He could see and understand both sides.

They have no control over their actions, Tarek realized. *They're just . . . driven. They don't know of any other way. Just to feed. Just to express the darkness within them—within us—through murder, the stealing of life. I want to kill. I need to. No! Stop it! You're thinking like one of them again. You're better than that. No, I'm not. Yes, you are. No, I'm not. Stop it. Stop it. Stop it! Give me something to drink. Shut your mouth! You don't want any. Mary looked so good. Sarah . . . so delicious. No! You're a fool. End this. Let them kill you. They know you're different. Die! Die! Die!*

The Bloodans came upon him, driving him into the dock's planks. He landed with a splash, his body spurting out in the shape of a star. He knew he was *disconnected,* knew that his arm was over there somewhere, his leg somewhere behind him. His other arm and leg somewhere in front and back. Even his head wasn't where it ought to be. Parts of his insides lay floating on the water beneath the dock, having slid through the cracks, slowly splitting apart.

Water. Hurry.

He pulled inward, imagining a cord running through his neck and limbs like mittens on a string. He pulled, tugged, pulled again, bringing his arms and legs and head back to his liquid torso. Drew up the dying parts of him floating on the water. It took longer than he felt it should, but once together, he never felt so whole, so complete. He was Tarek again. He was a Bloodan again. He was both.

A Bloodan on top of him drove its hand and arm into his back, the two liquid forms locking together. The creature pulled, forcing him up so he was on his feet. Another stood before him and kicked outward, its foot and shin landing in his gut with a wet suction sound as it also locked with him. Both creatures pulled, one tugging back, the other bending its knee fast and hard, pulling forward. Tarek thought he was going to split in two.

Has to be a way out. Has to. He didn't know how though, but then it came to him. He relaxed and let his body turn to goo, loose and liquidy, dripping—running—down off the arm behind him and the leg in front.

With a splash, he splayed out onto the planks, careful not to let any part of himself slip in between. He could sense the Bloodans were confused. *Got to get away. Got to feed. Mary and Sarah are over there. They smell so good.* Their scent was a fine red mist on the air. He looked on in wonder as the mist formed a trail leading up to the lodge. *They're over there. In there. Over there. Somewhere there.* Tarek rolled himself up and over, one end of him gaining ground, the other catching up from behind. He slithered away from the other Bloodans like a snake.

They followed.

Chapter Twelve
Home Again, Home Again

T HEY BLOCKED THE front doors with tables like before, but now joined by chairs, extra books and anything else heavy they could find placed on top. Mary and Sarah backed away from the doors, both keeping their eyes on them and to the windows to the side.

"Back in here again," Sarah said. She was still catching her breath from all the heavy lifting and pushing of tables.

"At least we're not outside," Mary said. "I'd rather be in here than anywhere else."

"I know I'm sounding like a broken record, but they'll come for us, you know."

"Yeah, I know. But I'd rather prolong it, if I could. There was . . ." She was about to mention the big Bloodan, the one that looked at her, the one that smiled. But she didn't quite know how to form the words.

She backed up against the far wall of the dining room and sank down, sitting with her forearms resting on her knees, her eyes never leaving the front doors.

"I wonder if they kill their own kind?" Sarah said.

Mary sat down beside her. "Who knows? I hope they do. But that big one, the one they're, what, killing? He, it, she—whatever—looked at me. I swear it did."

"They all look at us. They may not have eyes but they all look at us."

"I know, but this one . . . there was something in the way it looked at me. As if it was trying to say something." There had always been hate in a Bloodan's eyes when they stared at her. However, in the eyes of the big one . . .

The front doors shook as something large outside crashed against them. The two girls grabbed each other like frightened children.

Burm. Burm. Burm. The doors banged then shook, like thunder rumbling in the clouds.

Please don't come in, Mary thought.

The doors pulsed low and loud again, and then drummed its awful beat.

Burm. Burm. Burm. Bruduhduhduhduh. Burm. Burm. Burm. Bruduhduhduhduh. Mary felt the beat of the doors in her chest. The tables before the doors shook; the chairs pushed up against them teetered, then fell over along with the books on their seats. Then, with a loud *BOOM,* the two front doors opened a crack, shoving the tables forward, scraping them against the wooden floor, and bunching up the black carpet by their legs.

The two girls shot to their feet and bolted for the kitchen. Mary closed the door and peered out the circular window that oversaw the dining room and front doors.

BOOM! The front doors opened some more. Running along and up the side of one of them, a red film gelled and dribbled over, dripping onto a table in a thick stream of bloody syrup. The liquid moved across the tabletop and dripped to the floor on the other side. Once all of it was a huge puddle at the table's legs, it coalesced into a recognizable form.

A man made of red goo.

It was the big Bloodan.

Inside.

"Run," Sarah screamed.

She and Mary were at the door that led from the kitchen to the outside. They heard the Bloodan's wet body sliding along the ground as it traveled from the front doors to the swinging kitchen door no more than fifteen feet behind them. Mary paused while Sarah fumbled with the lock, trying desperately to open it, and saw the red goo bubbling beneath the doorframe, slipping in, and gathering into a thick pool of blood.

The puddle seemed to be looking at her.

"Got it," Sarah said as she got the lock open. "I wish this place didn't shift so much. The ground here . . . almost didn't—Mary? What—"

The pool of blood took on a humanlike form and towered above them.

"Mary!" Sarah screamed and grabbed her friend, drawing her toward the back door.

Mary turned to follow her out the back until she heard the Bloodan calling her name. Its voice was wet, slurred, like someone speaking through a mouth filled with water.

"Marryssh . . . pleeesh . . . it'shh meee . . . Tarexsh."

The words hit her hard. She didn't believe it; wouldn't believe it. The creature was lying. It had to be. But yet . . . it was different, wasn't it? The other creatures had attacked *it*. Moreover, this one *wasn't* attacking them now.

"It'sh meee, Marryssh. Pleeesh lishen."

A flicker of a face passed over the liquid red stare. "Tarek?" Mary heard herself say.

Just then, Sarah screamed and hurled pots and pans at the creature. Each pot and pan hit in splashes of red goo, splattering the walls and the surrounding countertops. There was nothing left of it, save for two liquid legs, standing there on their own. Then the blood on the counters and walls and floor gathered themselves and glided over to the legs, rolled up the calves, and built a human figure on top of them.

Sarah started to hurl another pan at it, but Mary stopped her. "It's no use. It'll just come back together again."

There was silence between the three for a long time. The thing never moved although Mary was prepared for it to lash out. However, Mary wasn't so sure if it was Tarek in front of her. Who knew what these creatures were capable of? They could very well have the ability to become, or at least be perceived as, someone else.

Yet, Tarek was their only hope for getting out alive.

They looked so beautiful to him, especially Mary. Perhaps because she had been the first person he came in contact with. Perhaps it was because he had seen her the most each time he made this jump to the past.

Mary, whose brown hair, dark eyes and curves would make any man, no matter what Time he was from, shudder with need.

Sarah was unbelievably gorgeous, too. She looked a lot like Mary but she didn't have that *something*, that sense of *yes,* Mary had. That something that just *clicked* when two people met.

For an instant, he thought he was in love with Mary, but he knew better. It wasn't his thoughts or feelings that caused this yearning for her. It was his hunger, a desire to feast upon the flesh and blood of a human, to merge with them, to become one with them.

He found himself moving forward, sliding along the floor toward Mary and Sarah. He could already feel himself connecting with them, using them, drawing their blood and satisfying his craving, his *need* of them. He stopped his advance when Mary and Sarah cowered back.

"I'm ssshorry," he said. "I didn'tsh meanssh to. I'm jusht . . . thirsshty." *So thirsty. So very thirsty. So . . . stop it! You're doing it again. Leave them be. Suffer, don't indulge. You're better than this.* But his thoughts brought him no comfort or encouragement. *Have to convince them I'm me. Have to let them know I'm a Blo—No . . . Tarek. They have to trust me. But can I trust myself?* He didn't have an answer.

The two girls looked puzzled, apparently unsure if their lives were over.

Have to get them to trust me.

He remembered the Tarek stolen by the Bloodans. He recalled what he looked like, what he wore, what he was before he died! No, not dead. He was still alive, wasn't he? He was still moving, still conscious and aware.

Relaxing his muscles, he let his shoulders slump, his back curve, let everything just relax. Blood rolled down the width of his back in a thick wave, moving downward and outwards, all the while running and dripping. The blood-wave elongated into a red sheet that hung from his shoulders to his ankles—just like his black cape once had. Red, bloody boots formed, rolled over at their cuffs. He focused on his face and for an instant, his attention already divided between his cape and boots, was able to form his face again, form *Tarek's* face. Then it was gone and only the cape and boots fashioned of blood remained.

He hoped it was enough for Mary to see who he was.

The two girls stared at him, eyes wide, and mouths hanging slightly open.

"Tarek?" Mary said.

Sarah looked like she was going to faint.

Chapter Thirteen
Reunited

THERE WASN'T MUCH time, he told them. The Bloodans were outside, trying to find a way in. The front doors to the mess hall were closed and the tables blocking it reinforced with a pot-filled island counter from the kitchen. Tarek, focusing on his blood-made hands, seeping them into the wood and using his incredible strength, managed to get the heavy kitchen island to the door without the girls' help.

The three were in the kitchen, away from the main door. The kitchen's back door was now secured with another counter.

"I thought you died," Mary said.

Tarek was on the far side of the room, a safe distance away. He didn't trust himself not to jump on the girls.

"I didsh, too," he said.

"What happened to you?" Sarah asked.

He remembered all too clearly. They had him surrounded, and without his gauntlet functioning, took him down within seconds. For the first time in a long time, he felt weak and ashamed at how much he relied on the machine attached to his forearm. Suddenly, two Bloodans were on top of him like cats on a mouse. His skin itched and pulled as they dug their way into him, driving themselves beneath his flesh, into his veins, into his muscles and bones—as they merged with him. He was warm and it was almost soothing, then he went cold, and worst of all, was confused. Red gloss blanketed his vision and his mind felt as if it was being sucked to someplace far away. Hope left him and the steady throbbing of his heart stilled. He was now dead yet he was still alive. He was now a Bloodan, one of them, one of the evil creatures he spent the majority of his life fighting, with only his hatred keeping him from losing himself completely. Rage bubbled in his veins, and all he wanted was to kill them. Then, out of nowhere except from perhaps somewhere deep within, behind what would be considered rational thought and feeling, an overwhelming feeling to *join* them, to promote their cause and assist them in the slaughtering of human beings, consumed him.

"I couldn't fightsh them," he said. "They weresh too shtrong. Too shtrong. Sho shtrong." He cast his gaze to the floor and his blood-like cape and boots diminished from his form. He was just like one of *them* again.

"I'm sorry," Mary said.

"For whatsh?" *You didn't do anything.*

"That they took you. That's two of us they got to, that are still . . . here. Me. You." She eyed Sarah. "You're the only one they haven't destroyed."

Sarah stood leaning against one of the cupboards. "Yeah, well, they better not."

A low rumble droned through the floorboards and two quick, booming thuds pulsed on the walls. The girls jumped.

"They're back," Mary said.

"Do you know how to beat them?" Sarah asked Tarek.

"Firesh. That'sh it. Blue flamesh. Watersh. Noshing elsh."

"The taps." She pointed to the sink.

Mary ran over to it and tried turning on the water. Only a short stream gushed out before the faucet went dry. "What the—" She got to her knees and checked the pipes in the cupboard beneath the sink. Everything seemed in place. "You don't suppose they turned the water off, do you?" She made a face. "Our water comes from the lake. That would mean they had done something to the plumbing that runs into it. Unearthed the pipe from the ground somewhere, maybe." She got to her feet. "Are you guys—I don't know—linked together or something? Do you know what they're thinking?"

Tarek shook his head. He ran his hand over his smooth scalp, appalled when all he felt was the scraping away of sticky goo. "They might be ablesh to know what eash ish thinkingsh. But I'm differensh. Maybe I'm outsh of the loopsh. I can shenshe them. Thatsh it. Don'tsh know whatsh they're thinkingsh." *I wish I did though. It would make this a lot easier. We can't just stay here. But where can we go? This whole place is contained inside some kind of bubble. I've never seen one before. I've heard of them, how they worked, heard of the Bloodans enclosing other soldiers' camps in domes, but rumors were all they were. Something from the other side of the world.*

The floor rumbled again and this time three loud thuds banged on the walls. Sarah yelped and Mary told her to be quiet. There was a scraping at the walls, growing louder, coming toward them. Sarah's yelp seemingly had alerted them to where they were in the mess hall.

The scraping grew louder and louder.

He didn't know how they'd survive the night.

Chapter Fourteen
Help

THE SCRAPING STOPPED just shy of the back door. Mary's heart was in her throat, Sarah was shaking, and Tarek was just . . . there. His blank, liquid-red face seemed to be looking in the direction of the doorway. No one moved.

The door rumbled and shook in its hinges as the counter in front of it vibrated on its legs. Mary knew Sarah and Tarek, like herself, were waiting for the door to burst open and a horde of Bloodans to come flooding in.

But none came. Not until Mary could swear there was nothing outside the back door, and all the droning thunder and rumbling and shaking of the door had all been her imagination.

Wood splintered everywhere and the door burst into slivers, shards of wood flying into the kitchen. The counter island flew from its place by the door and soared across the room, narrowly missing Sarah. The door handle made an awful screeching sound as it skidded along the floor. Mary and Sarah rushed to Tarek's side, and the three eyed the door.

Another boom and from somewhere behind them, past the kitchen, out in the dining area, the splintering of wood then the scraping of wooden shards as they slid across the floor.

The front door to the lodge had blown open.

The Bloodans could now come in from both sides.

There was no way out.

The three of them were finished.

The Bloodans came in, some sprinting in liquid strides, others sliding along the ground like snakes, still others oozing like melting wax on the doorframes. Behind the trio, the kitchen doors flew open hard, one of them knocked from its hinges, landing with a loud *thwump* upon the floor.

There were Bloodans on every side; a wall of red surrounded them.

Mary found it difficult to breathe. Sarah collapsed, her legs having given way beneath her.

Tarek just stood there, a red liquid cape forming along his body, boot cuffs taking shape just below his knees.

He's standing his ground, Mary thought. *So should I. So should we.* These thoughts suddenly gave her a sense of purpose, a boost of strength. It wasn't completely hopeless, even though there was no way the three of them could take on the forty or so creatures now in the room. Eyeing a few of them closer, some looked decidedly female.

The girls. Some of them were the girls, the campers she watched over this summer!

How can they hurt us? Mary didn't understand. If Tarek could control his hunger, his desire for prey, then couldn't the girls, as Bloodans, do so as well, or was he different?

The Bloodans closed in around them as Mary helped Sarah to her feet.

Just as they were about to strike, blue flame roared through the air, encompassing the room. Then a brilliant burst of white that faded into darkness.

Mary woke to a world of yellow flame. It took her a long while to adjust her eyes to what she was looking at.

A torch.

She followed its teardrop shape, the curves and points of yellow at its peak, the orange around its bell, the greeny-blue at its base. Beneath it was a wooden handle reminding her of the chair legs she and Sarah used when heading out to the bus.

The bus.

The girls made of blood.

The mess hall.

The kitchen.

Tarek.

Bloodans streaming in through the door.

A flash of white.

Beyond the torch's glow, a rugged-looking man with features cut from steel stared at her.

Mary screamed.

Chapter Fifteen
The Camp

"**R**ELAX, I WON'T hurt you," the man said.

Mary tried to restrain her whimpers, but to minimal success.

"Please, try to relax," he said. He withdrew the torch from close to her face and the absence of its heat sent a chill through her body.

"Wh-who are you?" she asked.

"My name is Salch," he said. "What is your name?"

What is *my name?* For a moment she couldn't remember. "M-Mary." The name sounded strangely foreign on her tongue.

Salch moved to the chair behind him and sat down, the torch's flame casting a soft glow on the small room they were in. The walls were made of rock, and a brown-like grit covered the stone of the floor. The entrance, some four feet from the bed she found herself lying on, led into a dark hallway. She sat up slightly, her head swimming from the sudden movement. She waited a moment to adjust and then sat up completely.

Salch looked . . . familiar. He wore dark trousers and a white shirt, frilly at the cuffs, the buttons leading up to the neck open, showing a well-muscled chest with little hair, glistening with sweat. His blond hair seemed to clash in contrast to the dark cape hanging off his shoulders. He wore dark boots rolled over at the cuffs, just below his knees. On his right forearm was a gleaming silver gauntlet.

Tarek.

He looked almost like Tarek before he became a . . .

"Tarek . . ." Mary said.

"You know him?" Salch said as he leaned forward in his chair.

"Where are we?" She swung her legs over the side of the bed and realized it wasn't a bed at all, more like a stone slab made up to look like a bed. It suddenly felt very hard and very cold.

"You're in our camp. We came just in time by the looks of it. They were about to kill you. There was a big one right beside you." Then, with a satisfied grin, "We left none alive."

Tarek? Oh no. Sarah. Where's . . . "Where's Sarah?"

"The girl that was with you? She's one room over, being attended to. She had a nasty fall when she dropped below the flames. It was only at the last moment we saw there were people in the room with the pots and pans, right before we opened fire." Salch spoke with a calm resolve that Mary found unsettling, as though violence was commonplace in his life. "Opened fire," he had said, no differently than one would say they got out of bed and combed their hair that morning. "You said you knew Tarek," he finished.

"He was with us when you . . . you came in and—What happened?"

Mary listened as Salch revealed the details of what happened in the kitchen at Camp Silverway. He said he and his men were out on the field in battle when suddenly they saw a window on the air and the Bloodans in "the room with the pots and pans" —he apparently didn't know the word "kitchen" —and opened fire, trying to kill as many Bloodans as they could. He also said there were more outside the room with the pots and pans and he and three other men got rid of the threat. He repeated they left none alive.

Then that would mean Tarek is dead. He was one of them, part of the same, what, army, as Salch's? How could they kill one of their own? But they didn't know it was Tarek, did they? He was a Bloodan. They kill Bloodans. All dead. All of them. Confusion set in like that day long ago, not understanding what was going on while a Bloodan sucked the life out of Shelly. Her entire life seemed to revolve around Bloodans and what they did to people. There seemed to be no escape from them. *I am a victim, aren't I? No way out. Just me and them and all this screwy stuff that doesn't make sense, yet seems to make sense all the same. Bloodans and fire and Bloodans and fire and Bloodans and fire and on and on, here we go, so messed up so.*

"Where are we?" she asked again.

"You're in our camp. I already said that."

Geez, sorry. Have some compassion. She felt bitchy, probably due to lack of sleep. Bitchy and incredibly tired. She didn't know how long she had been out for. "What time is it?"

"Time?"

"Yes, time. What time is it? Two in the morning, three? You can't be that clueless."

Salch let out a laugh, as if he enjoyed her moodiness. "It's early into the new day, if that's what you mean. I'm not sure of the hour. You were only unconscious for a short while."

"How long?"

"A short while."

He doesn't even know what time it is. "When can I see Sarah?"

"Right now if you'd like. I just need to go check if she's awake. Give me a moment." When he stood, she was amazed at how tall he was. He had to dip his head so as to not hit it against the low ceiling. Guessing, Mary thought he'd be almost seven feet when standing upright.

However, when he left, whether intentional or not, he took the torch with him, leaving her alone in the dark.

The two girls were alone in Mary's tiny room after Salch brought Sarah over. Thankfully, a torch was left for them in an iron holder on the stone wall.

"We have to get out of here," Sarah said.

Seems like that's all we've been saying, Mary thought. She looked Sarah over and noticed a bump on her head and a treated cut over her eye. She told Mary it was a man dressed like Salch, who didn't give her his name, that had bandaged it.

"Do you know where we are?" Mary asked. "Salch never told me anything."

"Salch?"

"The guy who woke me."

"Oh. No, not really. The guy who put this bandage on me didn't talk. Not once despite how many questions I asked." A scowl creased her face. Her shoulders sagged. "He was dressed like Tarek."

"Same with Salch."

"Do you suppose—" Sarah glanced elsewhere past Mary, as if seeking permission from something unseen, to whisper, "We aren't at Camp Silverway anymore?"

Not at Camp Silverway! Then she realized exactly what Sarah meant. Salch had said she was in *his* camp.

Camp.

The war.

Man versus Bloodan.

Tarek's world.

"No, we can't be. Time travel . . . it's impossible!" *But that isn't true, either, is it? Tarek came to Camp Silverway, twice!*

Just then Salch came into the room. "I hope you ladies are comfortable." He sat down on the stool next to the stone bed. "Now, tell me," he continued, "where's Tarek?"

Chapter Sixteen
Fighting

"**H**E'S ONE OF them now," Mary said. "He's a Bloodan."

"It's true," Sarah added. "But we're not entirely sure, either. Can Bloodans *become* other people?"

Salch sighed. "No. Not that I've seen, and I've been at this a long time."

How long? Mary wondered. *He looks aged by a hard life, but he can't be, what, no more than thirty-five years old, forty?*

"Are you certain it was him?" Salch said.

Mary thought back to Tarek and the liquid red cape hanging off his back, the blood-colored folds that were the boot cuffs beneath his knees. "It had to be. He looked just like he did as a . . . as a man . . . but he was all red, like a Bloodan. He had a cape made of blood. Boots, too."

"You should have killed him," Salch said. "I don't know how he was still able to be himself, but even so, he's dangerous. The Bloodan within him, it will soon control him. He'll die—the part of him that's still Tarek, that is—but not before killing as many as he can. He's Bloodan now. No more, no less."

"He didn't attack us," Sarah said. "He saved us from the others. He didn't hurt us."

Salch's sharp gaze settled on Sarah. "Not yet. But he will. Like I said, you should have killed him."

"With what?" Mary asked. "That thing of his? The thing that shoots blue fire? It was broken before he even became a Bloodan. We tried using torches, he showed us which part of the flame hurt a Bloodan, but we didn't have any torches when he came to us, so we couldn't have killed him even if we wanted to. And he also found out water kills Bloodans, too, but we didn't have any of that either."

Salch didn't seem pleased with her answer, but there was nothing he could say. His nose whistled when he exhaled. "Water, huh? Tarek is smart," Salch continued. "One of the best I've seen in this war. If my men haven't killed him along with the other Bloodans and he's still alive, and if he has returned with us to our world, then either he's already joined the other Bloodans, or he'll be on his way back here, seeking protection. But, as I said, he's smart. He might just choose to wander off alone, away from both man and Bloodan alike."

"The creatures knew he was different," Mary said. "They tried to kill him."

"Then all the more reason he should hide. Now he's got two sides looking for him."

A short while later, Salch led Mary and Sarah out of the small room and down the dark hallway, the only light coming from the torch he carried. The brown rock around them, cast in an orange tone, reminded her of descriptions of Hell. *Is that where I am now?*

The hallway twisted and turned. At last they walked up a steep rocky slope and at the top was an iron door. Salch pulled out a key from the pouch on his belt and undid the lock. Mary braced herself for the onslaught of daylight once the door opened. However, when he opened the door, no light flooded in.

The sky beyond was red, with patches of charcoal black. A thick gray smoke hung on the air, the sharp smell stinging her nostrils.

This can't be real, she thought. They came out onto a smoke-veiled rocky plain. Salch closed the iron door and locked it.

He drew up beside them. "Welcome to my world," he said.

Tarek was far from Salch's camp. How he longed to go there, to be in the comforting presence of his peers—but he couldn't, not anymore. He was neither human nor monster, but some kind of unholy hybrid.

Am I? I'm one of them, yet— There was no hope. *At least I made it back through. I got out of the room with the pots and pans easily enough. Just relaxed, turned to a pool of goo, avoided the fire, and slid out. The Veil had been opened. Don't know how Salch and his men found us. Those portals are rare. The last one aside from . . . wait. No. Something . . . they're . . . common? When I first saw Mary . . .*

The back of his throat suddenly dried up. Or, something like it.

He was thirsty.

"Where are we?" Sarah asked.

"You're where *your* camp once was long ago. I don't know how much Tarek told you, but the Bloodans are able to rip open the seals of an era, create a doorway, as it were, to someplace—to some *time*—else."

"You mean we're in the—in the future?" It was obvious to Mary that Sarah didn't believe it. She was having a hard time believing it herself. What was once thought of as *unreal* and *impossible* no longer had meaning. They were in the future, plain and simple.

"Why did you bring us outside?" Mary asked Salch.

"Because you would have asked me to bring you up here eventually. Girls don't like spending a long time in holes in the ground," he said.

What! "What is that supposed to mean?"

"It means—"

The sound of low, thick whispers filled the air as the smoke around them began to take on a tint of red. That all-too-familiar scraping sound rose up as well.

The Bloodans were coming.

"Quick, get indoors!" he said as he sprang for the iron door and fumbled for the key to unlock it.

Mary and Sarah huddled up beside him, and there, coming at them through the smoke, were the shadows of Bloodans, their stride ever quickening.

Salch got the door open and the girls ran inside. Beside the door, just inside the entrance, was a bell, which Mary hadn't noticed when they first passed. He reached in, rang the bell, and its sound echoed throughout the hallway and into the caves below.

In the dark tunnel, men shouted, the echo of their boots clopping on stone. Soon the light from torches shone against the walls. Then dark capes. Then white shirts. Then silver gauntlets.

It was a relieving sight. Sarah and Mary moved out of the way and back out of the cave entrance to let the men pass. The combined sound, that oh-so-good sound of so many gauntlets powering-up, filled Mary's ears and her heart beat quickly with the hope of survival.

The moment the first soldier came out of the torch-lit hallway, a Bloodan's cry mixed with Salch's ringing of the bell. The creature flew toward the soldier. As other men came out into the open, the soldier under attack fired off a ball of blue flame. The flame pierced the creature and sent it reeling into scattered drops of blood.

Yes! Mary cheered silently.

The Bloodan reassembled itself as more creatures emerged from the smoke.

The fight was on.

Chapter Seventeen
War

THE AIR SUDDENLY came alive with blue fire and red liquid, as flame and Bloodan collided in every direction Mary looked. She tried desperately to find Salch in all this, but he was nowhere in view.

"Mary, come on!" It was Sarah, standing by the doorway that led underground.

What can I— Mary was torn as to what to do. A part of her wanted to stay and fight, the other wanted to flee.

"Mary!" Sarah was already beneath the doorframe, waving for her to come inside.

Mary ducked instinctively as a ball of fire zipped past, narrowly missing her. The screeching of Bloodans was everywhere as was the soothing powering-up sound from not just one, but many gauntlets.

"I'm not going to keep this door open much longer!" There were tears in Sarah's eyes.

Mary moved toward her . . . then stopped.

"I-I . . . I can't," she said. "I'm sorry." *I have to stay. If I hide . . . if I hide, it'll be just like before—running from the past. Can't go on like this. Must end it. Have to.*

"Mary, please, listen to me," Sarah said, "you have to come inside." Then, "Mary, look out!"

A Bloodan appeared out of the smoke and landed on top of her.

"Mary!" Sarah screamed, her voice thick with tears.

The awful, blank liquid stare of the creature loomed just inches from Mary's face. She saw her reflection in its mirror-like surface. She tried to push the Bloodan off her, but her hands kept sliding on its gel-like body, her fingers kneading into it instead of gripping it.

"Help!" she screamed.

The loud *ka-chunk* of iron on rock played in her ears. Sarah closed the door.

She . . . she left me. No! Please, save me!

With a low rumble in its throat, the Bloodan's face pressed ever closer to hers.

All Mary could manage were whispering sobs. "No, no, no, no . . ."

All at once, Mary felt a hot sensation throughout her body as the Bloodan began to seep into her.

No . . . don't take me . . . no . . . Her eyes squeezed shut and her fingers dug into the Bloodan's liquid skin. She released her hands the moment she felt it surge into her even further. Gripping had only encouraged it.

She dare not open her eyes. She didn't want to see nothing but red, didn't want to acknowledge the creature. After all the running, the hiding, the escaping from it, not just at Camp Silverway, but in her own life for years. She didn't want to come to terms that she failed.

Apathy set in, and her body relaxed.

Soon, she would be gone.

Whoomph.

Sccrrreeeeeeaaaaahhhhh.

Whoomph.

So cold. Freezing. Utterly frozen, the heat from the Bloodan sinking into Mary had left. Was this it? Had she become one of them? Was this how it was when you died? Cold? Alone? Helpless? No God or Angels? Not even Hell?

Whoomph.

Sccrreeaahh . . .

Sploosh.

Silence.

Mary opened her eyes.

The sky above was a mixture of red and black clouds. There was gray smoky mist all around her. She coughed, swallowed, and then coughed again. She sat up, leaned on her elbows, and jolted when Salch came up from behind.

"Let's go," he said and grabbed her by the arm, pulling her up hard. Her feet almost came out from under her from the force.

"Ow."

Salch gripped her head, her cheekbones in his palms. He eyed her like a doctor checking someone's tonsils.

"What—?" she started.

"Silence."

Fire whooshing and Bloodans screaming filtered through the fog. Salch's stare was like iron.

Why's he looking at me like that? she wondered.

His palms squeezed harder on her cheeks. Mary whimpered and a tear rolled along one side of her nose. Just when she thought he would keep pressing until her head caved in, he released her. Her hands immediately went to cradle her cheeks.

"You're clean," he said, and the moment his eyes drifted past her to something beyond, he shouted, "Get down!"

He threw her to the ground. She bruised her elbows and skinned her hands. Bursts of blue flashed somewhere above her and a Bloodan roared as it splashed into thousands of red droplets.

The squishy sound of the Bloodan reassembling itself was annihilated by another ball of blue fire.

Tarek's words from when she first met him filled her ears. *One for warning, two for glory.*

Mary got to her feet as Salch tucked his gauntlet away beneath his cape. "How many are there?" she asked.

"Thrice as many as there are people. The reason why there's only a few out front of the bunker, is my men drew them out into the smoke, obscuring the Bloodans' sight and sense of smell. But they come here. They know this is one of our hiding places. However, they also know that to get in, they would have to thin their numbers due to a doorway only being able to handle so many. They realize that our guards would be on them quickly, killing them two or three at a time. They would have to stop their advance." He ran a hand over his forehead, pushing back sweaty bangs. "Regardless, they come. They try to draw us out. The only reason we play along is to kill them."

"Play along," Mary said. "Tarek said nearly the same thing. He said this is all a game to them. Now I see this whole war is a game."

"But a game that should be played, don't you think?" He put one arm around her and with a sweep of the other, gestured to the smoky air. "All this would be lost if we didn't play. Smoke can rise and eventually disappear and the world can be rebuilt. I don't want to live in a cave for the rest of my life. Nor do I want my children to, or their children, or their children still. It all has to end if humanity is to survive. Yes, my dear, it is a game well worth playing."

Chapter Eighteen
Resurfacing

T AREK CONCEALED HIMSELF as best he could, shielding his red form in the smoke-laden air, getting as far from the battle as possible. Everyone was looking for him. Bloodans and humans alike. Well, they weren't exactly *looking* for him, but should they come across him, he was as good as dead.

To go back. To be a man once more. To fight the very thing I've become. The very thing I hate. Yet . . .

There was a spark of hope; something kept him going and made him want to live. He *was* hiding, protecting himself, after all.

He thought about returning home, but then remembered his home was a camp shared with the men he once led. Could he approach them, explain what happened? Could he trust them to recognize him for who he was and not kill him at first sight? His men were trained to kill any and all things red. That was why no human who fought in this war wore red. The color was hated, and it assured that the soldiers were not mistaken for Bloodans from a distance. The capes also added to this, separating the men from the creatures even more, when only silhouettes against the smoke could be seen.

The girls. Mary. Sarah. Where are they? Tarek thought. *Salch's camp. That's right. He took them from the room with the pots and pans.* With a heavy heart and mind, Tarek took one step forward. Then another, and another, disappearing into the smoke.

It was time to set things right. He had to. He knew he couldn't go on like this, having no one. But how he would right the situation, he didn't know. Yet, he also knew how his mind worked. At least, how *Tarek's* mind worked. Things were different now. Nevertheless, he was still the same underneath the blood, the liquid, the desire to sink into humans and merge with them—wasn't he? He hoped so. He needed it to be so.

The smoke thinned enough for him to see more clearly, as if looking through a veil of bloody liquid, like a red waterfall captured in stillness, wasn't hard enough as it was. Sometimes he wished his mind to be separated from what he was. Other times he was thankful he was still himself. Mostly, anyway.

The silhouettes of Bloodans graced the blanket of smoke, the creatures darting in disorder; bursts of fire zipped through the air and the creatures' screams were the only sound. Standing upright, he glided along the uneven terrain like water running over rocky crags and crevices.

A bright light came toward him. He ducked and the searing heat of flame rushed by overhead. Fire seemed even hotter, now that he was one of them. He didn't know why that was but something inside told him it had to do with now being part of a place that wasn't . . . Earth . . . but somewhere far below. Maybe even somewhere that was *elsewhere.*

"Get them!" someone shouted. Tarek recognized the voice as belonging to Chaz, Salch's second-in-command.

More balls of fire lit up the smoke like lightning on clouds. More screams and squeals spewed from the Bloodans' mouths.

Suddenly, a Bloodan appeared out of the smoke, crashing into him, their bodies immediately merging. He felt the very sharp and very real intrusion of the creature's gooey form.

He focused himself, gripped the creature, and squeezed so tight, the Bloodan's limbs—an arm and a leg—began to withdraw from his body like a hand being squeezed out of a handshake.

The Bloodan recoiled backward and Tarek got to his feet. The Bloodan was up in no time as well, hatred in its red face.

Snapping his arm outward, his fist punched through the creature's head and gripped something tingling within. Its brain, perhaps? Regardless, the creature fell to its knees, its legs splashing as they made contact with the ground. The Bloodan moaned and Tarek squeezed that *thing* inside its head even harder. Soon the Bloodan melted into a pool of dark red and didn't reassemble itself. The Bloodan was dead.

If death is even possible for those like me—for those like them, he thought.

"Run back! Run back!" shouted another soldier, one whose voice Tarek didn't recognize. A shadow scampered across the cloudy air.

I wonder where Mary and Sarah are? I hope they are safe.

Flames lit up the gray around him and flashed against the sky, the blue mixing with the red, creating an instant of purple flare.

Three Bloodans were spotted heading toward a shadow that *had* to be a man. The silhouette of a cape twirled for a moment.

Tarek charged toward them.

With torch in hand, Sarah cautiously stepped out of the bunker and onto the battleground.

"Mary?" was her first word. She couldn't see her friend anywhere.

Oh no. I don't want to be alone. Why did I go back inside? Please, help me. Then, *Who are you talking to?* It was still her voice, but more of an echo. *I need to find someone. Where's that guy? Satch? No, wait, Salch. Yeah, that's the one. Where is he? Crap, crap, crap.*

Heart racing, she stepped ever so slowly, careful to be as quiet as possible so none of the creatures would hear her. No one was around. No shadows, no sound, no anything. Just smoke.

"Hello?" Her voice was weak, frail, like a child waking up to find no one in the house. "Crap."

She waded further into the smoke. Waded and walked. *Waited* then walked. She glanced at the flame she carried: a torch from one of those iron holders on the wall inside the cave. She hoped it didn't burn out before she had to use it. *If* she had to use it. *I hope not.*

A scream to the right. A *female* scream. Mary!

Sarah ran in that direction.

Tarek had taken the three Bloodans down. He was getting used to reaching inside their heads, squeezing that ever-so-precious tingling matter within and killing them almost instantly. Aside from that little slip up with his final victim, he thought he was getting quite good at it, and was beginning to enjoy killing them. Just like he had when he was fully human.

Out of the smoke, a Bloodan dropped from above and landed before him. He noticed the creature's feet splashed when they hit the ground but soon reformed themselves. It moved toward him. Tarek relaxed his hand, shot his arm outward, passed his fingers through the Bloodan's head and clutched that electrifying thing within. The creature bellowed and was dead before it could realize what happened.

"Finallleeesh," he said. "Onlysh one for gloreeesh. Yesh. No warningsh."

He continued on into the thick of the battle. Each Bloodan that came after him, he destroyed. He kept himself concealed from the soldiers running about, dodging the fireballs that came his way. Each time one passed, even if it was within only a few feet of him, the heat coming off the balls of fire was enough for him to jerk in the opposite direction, his body boiling from the pain. He was amazed at how fast he recovered, but he also knew that each dodge of flame made him more weary.

"Mary? You here?" Sarah could have sworn she heard a woman scream.

Just then, the muscles at the back of her neck tensed and her calves seemed to have lost all sturdiness. Something wasn't right. The moment she turned around, four Bloodans were on top of her. Before her body hit the ground, one was already digging its way into her skin. The torch fell and rolled away, lost to the smoke.

There was a mound of them, all piled up on something. How many were there? Tarek thought he saw only three. *No problem. Just reach, squeeze, and it's over.*

He bounded toward the mound like a wolf after a rabbit. He killed two of them at the same time, both hands gripping their tingling brains. The third jumped on top of him, its liquid legs landing on his shoulders, then sinking downward into his torso, like slipping into a second skin. Tarek wailed and his whole body tensed. Glancing up, the look upon the Bloodan's face told him it felt the discomfort, too, but not nearly to the same extent he felt.

He reached his arms around the back of the creature and slid in his fists. He let his hands merge with the creature's shoulder blades, and with a hard push he pressed outward, slowly separating himself and the creature. The Bloodan tried to push itself back into him, but he resisted.

His hands pounded from the Bloodan's weight, feeling as though he'd soon lose his grip; he pushed back harder. His shoulders heated with strain and his back ached. Then, with a shrill yell, he exerted one final blast of effort and pressed out fast and hard, throwing the creature away from him. He immediately withdrew his hands and dug both of them into the creature's head, putting pressure on the electrifying thing inside.

You'll never kill again, he thought as the creature fell to its knees and soon shrank to a melting, gooey ball.

Tarek felt as though he should catch his breath and realized he didn't need to breathe. He saw another Bloodan on the ground, nearly completely submerged in a human being.

Mary! Tarek went over and upon closer inspection he saw it wasn't Mary; it was Sarah.

With powerful, gel-like hands, he reached into the merging form.

"Come onsh. Noosh. Can'tsh diesh. Not yetsh." *Please, let her be all right. Pull. PULL!* Grunting, he tried separating the Bloodan from Sarah. It was too late. The creature was too far *in*.

"Noooooooosh!" Tarek wailed. *Can't fail her. Can't. Never, never, never.*

But he had. The Bloodan had complete rule over Sarah's body.

Behind him, Tarek heard the all-too-familiar powering-up sound of a gauntlet.

Chapter Nineteen
The Past Appears

Mary became separated from Salch when a Bloodan burst out of the smoke and, just as quickly, dragged him back into it. No matter where she searched, she could not find him. She was alone.

Only out here, in an atmosphere of smoke and beneath a red sky, did she understand what that truly meant. Even on those lonely nights in her apartment back in the city, hiding beneath her sheets, images of Shelly being forcefully consumed by a Bloodan dancing in her mind—none of it compared to the heavy solitude she now felt.

All around her were the screams of both men and Bloodan. Small, rocky hill-like boulders appeared every now and again as she wandered through the smoke. She was trying to find her way back to Salch's cave but was hopelessly turned around. She approached two more boulders and leaned up against them. Smoke stinging her eyes, she wiped the tears away with her sleeve. Was it just her, or did the smoke seem thinner over here and the land more red? Glancing up at the blood-red sky affirmed her thought.

Blood.

Death.

Bloodans.

Damn. She hated those things. They stole her life, made her obsess over them, consumed by them.

With hand and foot, she tested the boulder's surface and found it had enough cracks for her to grip and used them to climb up. Once atop the boulder, it was as if she was on an island amidst a sea of gray water. Below, the smoke stirred, rose, settled, and moved everywhere.

How long have they been fighting? she wondered. *For a long time, it seems. Just look at Tarek and Salch. Two men, aged and hard from battle. Sheesh, Mary. You sound like someone out of an old war novel.*

When she wiped more tears from her sore eyes, she saw shadows swimming in the smoke. The shadows grew darker, their tint changing from deep gray to brick-red—to blood.

Six Bloodans sprung out of the mist and landed on top of the rocky, boulder-made hill where she stood. She screamed and tried to jump off and run away, but a Bloodan caught her the moment her leg moved and held her tight. The wet body was already soaking through her clothes and moistening her skin, while two others hopped onto the hill.

For a brief moment, Mary's heart stopped.

The powering-up sound sent shivers through Tarek. He peered over his shoulder and saw Salch standing over him, shiny silver gauntlet pointed at his head, the residue of previous flames giving off a salty scent from the tip.

Salch stood there, keeping his firearm on Tarek, but he did not shoot. If anything, there seemed to be hesitation in his gaze, as though he knew this wasn't just some Bloodan before him, but something else.

And Tarek realized why. He saw his own liquid red cape swirling about him, boot cuffs folded and scrunched beneath his bended knees. And yes, he could see it between his eyes, the faint shadow of a nose. It was red, but it was still his. Had Salch saw his face?

"Salssh . . ." Tarek said.

The gauntlet remained poised at him. Tarek's cape rippled, and he realized he was controlling it, as though a part of him like an arm or leg.

"I wash too latesh," Tarek said.

The Bloodan—Sarah—sat up, set its gaze on Tarek, and lunged. Before the creature could make contact, she was blown back in a hailstorm of flame that burned Tarek's body. Several feet away she splashed against the ground. When she reformed herself and came back at Tarek and Salch, she shrieked as she dove through the air. Another ball of fire silenced her, destroyed her.

"One for warning, two for glory," Salch said. The gauntlet fell back on Tarek.

"Salssh, pleeesh. Don'sht shootsh." *Please don't.* Yet, a part of him *wanted* Salch to open fire. Death would end the conflict within. *No. Have to keep fighting. Damn!*

The gauntlet powered up again.

As the Bloodan clutched its arm around Mary's throat, something . . . strange . . . began to happen. Her foot moved slightly; there was a sloshing sound and she realized she was standing in a puddle. A puddle made of blood. In fact, the whole hill was soaked in it.

More Bloodans rose up around her.

Why don't they kill me? she wondered.

Then she saw why. Above the Bloodans, a shiny, liquid, semi-transparent disc formed, blending with the red sky. Blood bubbled and boiled on the rock, Mary's soles dancing because of the heat, yet it did not burn her.

The disc spun like a record moving swiftly on a turntable, lifting higher above them, turning itself on an arc so that it faced them, up against the rock. The circle, still spinning, must have been ten feet tall, if not a foot or two more. Red smoke and running blood swirled and twirled, faster and faster, moving in and out of itself, like a funnel's flow being constantly reversed.

A wave of blood swept across it and the circle closed in on itself, left to right, and became a red slit, like a snake's eye turned on its side. The transparent liquid within shimmered and rolled in on itself and Mary saw Camp Silverway through the opening.

Mary recalled what Tarek said about this "doorway." The evil inside the Bloodans could open it. Whether they could create it intentionally or not, she wasn't sure. Death. Bloodshed. Murder.

Now I'm going to die, she thought as the Bloodans closed in.

Tarek knocked the gauntlet away and Salch stumbled back. Kicking out, keeping his liquid form together, he spun and swept Salch's legs out from under him. The gauntlet clanged against the rocky terrain. As Salch landed on his back, hard, Tarek jumped on top of him.

Drink. Yes, drink. Kill. Salch is mine. All mine. Yes. So hungry. Give me. Give me. Now. Now. STOP! Remove the gauntlet. Relax. Don't give in. But he so badly wanted to give in, to feast. He needed nourishment. Needed to *merge.*

Salch's arm bent at the elbow, trying to point the gauntlet at Tarek's head. Tarek slid his hand down Salch's arm and with a hard push, removed the gauntlet. It was then he fully understood he was stronger than the other Bloodans. None of the others had ever removed a gauntlet from a soldier. None that he was aware of, anyway.

Eyes wide, Salch licked his lips. "Go on. Kill me. End it now."

No, friend. Yes! Already Tarek was separated from his old self and he was leaning in, his forehead about to connect with Salch's, ready to merge. Oh, to sink into him. How good it would feel to be filled up. To fill *Salch* up. To become one with him. *Never!* Tarek backed off from his friend.

Salch only stared at him, wide-eyed, but soon a hateful grimace creased his face.

"I'm sorrysh," Tarek said. "I—Sorrysh. I'm sshtill learningsh controlsh. Sho hardsh."

The former human turned away, listening as Salch got to his feet.

A human fist penetrated Tarek's back. It didn't hurt. Not at all.

His muscles—if you could call them that—locked up. He gripped the fist by squeezing his shoulder blades together, then spun around and mauled the soldier behind him. Within an instant, Tarek was already merging with the soldier. This nameless human. It wasn't Salch; he merely looked on. The soldier did look familiar though, but Tarek was so far lost in the merging that he didn't care who it was. Nothing mattered. Just merge, merge, and blend into this wretch of a creature, this human.

Skin touched blood; blood touched skin, sinking, traveling inward, seeping through pores like water through potholes. Oh, heavenly, glorious, orgasmic. Drink, eat, become this person, take them away and erase their existence from this planet. Rebuild and renourish. Drink, friend, drink.

A boot in Tarek's side. Salch's boot. Tarek gripped him, tensing that spot between ribs and waist. He torqued his body to the left and hurled Salch several feet away.

Leave me! Don't disturb me. I am . . . I am invincible! Tarek's thoughts raced, not just in his head but also in his whole being. His mind awakened to the soldier's brain, understanding the soldier's thoughts and feelings and emotions of fear and surrender. *No. Can't. Yes. No more fighting. I hate me!* Tarek tried to pull himself away from the human, but it felt as though the human was pulling *him* in. *Must . . . release . . . if you give in, you're no better. Better off to die starving and alone than become a filthy Bloodan all the way.*

Salch, a red-purple bruise on his cheek, ran toward them.

The soldier wiggled and squirmed beneath Tarek.

Merge . . .

Tarek finally gave in to the Bloodan inside him. He couldn't help it.

Just as the thought of death struck Mary, she saw someone through the slit that, moments ago, revealed Camp Silverway. The camp was dark.

Must be night, she thought, stating the obvious. The shadow of a person ran, growing wider and larger in the opening as it neared. However, there was more to this silhouette than just arms and legs. Something moved behind it, something flat, fluid. One arm looked bigger than the other. The red slit separating Time grew to become a disc again. Lightning struck and heat became everything. Bloodans screeched and Mary fell to her knees as a ball of blue flame raced above her.

Blood splashed all around her and the Bloodans reformed themselves, the blood on her skin leaving her and rejoining with their masters' liquid red forms. Another blast of fire and the Bloodans blew apart in a shower of red droplets.

The disc swirled faster and faster and faster still. Then, quickly, faded away.

Mary gasped and caught her breath. She didn't know when she had dropped on all fours.

"Who are you?" came a low voice above her.

Mary's heart lightened when she realized who it was.

Tarek.

Chapter Twenty

Two

M ARY EYED TAREK from his brown boots all the way up his muscled body, past the white ruffles of his shirt, to the strap that held his cape across his chest and the glint of silver on his right arm—his gauntlet—up to his chiseled face and icy blue stare. His brown hair ruffled in the wind the disappearing disc created.

"Answer me!" His gauntlet powered up. "All women are to stay indoors. If your husband knew you were out here . . . . The very survival of our race depends on you women."

"T-Tarek?" she said, still on her hands and knees.

"How do you know my name?" His brow furrowed, and he made a face as though responding to something offensive. "I've never seen you before."

She slowly got up, Tarek's gauntlet on her all the while. *Where did he come from?* It took her a moment to understand. *That disc. A window. The . . . past?*

"Where were you?" she asked.

"None of your business. Now, come with me. We have to get inside. An Escape Shelter is not far from here." He eyed the Bloodans he had just destroyed. "You're very lucky that Veil opened up when it did. You would have been one of them by now."

"Veil?" *The disc!*

Tarek gripped her face in his large hands, examining her, just as Salch had, also squeezing just as hard, if not harder still. "You're clean," he said after he was done.

That's twice, now. She sighed.

Her legs were shaky as he led her off the boulders and across the rocky terrain. She couldn't see anything through the gray smoke swirling around them, yet he walked with ease, as though it was a clear sunny day.

"They took you," she said.

"Quiet. You don't want them to hear you." He scanned the mist around them.

She raced in front of him, nearly tripping over a rock but managing to retain her balance, and stood before him. "Listen to me! The Bloodans took you! You became one of them! I swear it. You're . . . a Bloodan."

Fire and rage lit his eyes, his left hand rising, about to swat her. "How dare you call me that! You're fortunate I don't break your jaw for saying such a thing!"

"You have to believe me. You saved a friend and me from those things at Camp Silverway, where you just were. We somehow wound up here. A doorway opened, one of those disc things."

He paused and his hand slowly lowered. Tarek strode past her.

"I met Salch," she called after him.

Tarek stopped. "Salch? How do you know him? Are you one of his women?"

"I was in his cave. He brought me and my friend, Sarah, there, and tended to our wounds. Tarek, you must believe me. None of this makes sense. I saw them turn you into a Bloodan. You *are* one of them. You have to be. Unless . . . unless . . ." And then it became clear.

Tarek spun on his heels and marched toward her, grabbing her arm hard and swift.

"You're coming with me," he said, dragging her along.

Wait! Now I get it. But . . . it's impossible. Yet, it is possible, isn't it? The doorway to the past. How Tarek hadn't changed a day when he returned to Camp Silverway. How the Bloodans got in.

"I'm sorry," she said.

His grip on her bicep eased a little, but he still held her strong.

"I understand what happened. You're not a Bloodan." *Not yet,* she added to herself. "And I hope you never will be. I'm sorry."

He let go of her arm and walked alongside her, a few steps to her right.

"You went to the past," she said, "to kill a Bloodan. You followed it." *Please, believe me.*

Tarek eyed her skeptically.

"You broke open the door to a cabin and saved a girl in a lower bunk from one that was sinking into her. There was another girl there, crying on the top bunk in the middle of the room. The brown hair hanging over her eyes made it difficult for you to see her face. But she saw you."

"How do you know what happened?" Was that a hint of fear in his voice? She couldn't tell.

Mary stopped her stride. "Because," she said, "I was there. The girl crying . . . that was me."

Memories ran through the Bloodan—Tarek—like a swift current, ransacking all that he was, and all he had been before he became a Bloodan. Thoughts of fear—Salch's thoughts—became his only consciousness for a time. Emotions of hope, war, victory, defeat and death all came crashing down as he merged with Salch.

It was over. It had been done. Tarek was a Bloodan.

He had killed.

Despite the blessed relief the merging with Salch brought, Tarek rued his actions and for a long time remained on his knees, yearning for a chance to turn back Time. He longed for a Veil to come along that would open up to the time when he had leaned over Salch and was about to feast. He would stop himself, he knew, should the opportunity ever come about and to hell with the pain afterward from not feeding.

I need to make this right. I never knew my fate could be one such as this. His thought brought red tears to his eyes. The moment they fell, they rolled partway down his cheek and were absorbed back into his skin.

Let them take me. Man, Bloodan, I don't care. Hope is lost. I have failed.

Tarek stood and, head bowed, made his way toward the battle, not caring when he fell.

Walking with Mary brought with it a strange feeling. Tarek had just met her—really met her—only moments ago, but he felt as if he had met her before. Maybe what she said was true? Maybe she was that little girl, the one whose cries made his heart weep? It was possible. Time travel was possible, but random, or an accident. The Bloodans started it, their evil ripping open a hole in Space and Time, leaving a doorway for anyone near to travel through. He was fortunate that he found a doorway back from Camp Silverway. But he also knew the cause of that doorway had been the Bloodans that were around Mary on those boulders, and that he arrived just in time.

"Where are we going?" Mary asked.

"Some place safe. There's Escape Shelters hidden all over, but still far enough away from our main strongholds, like the one you were in with Salch. We'll hide in a Shelter until the battle clears. You shouldn't even be out here to begin with, no matter *when* you're from." He put a hand to her shoulder, stopping her. "Wait."

Gauntlet raised, Tarek eyed the smoke. *The bastards . . . they're . . .* Blue fire zipped from the gauntlet's tip and flickered as it disappeared into the smoke. A moment later, there was a haunting scream and he knew he had hit his target. He fired again, knowing that when one of them reformed, it always gathered itself in the same spot it once stood. Another moment passed and a fowl screech echoed in the distance.

"How did you know it was there?" Mary asked.

"I knew," he said. The two walked on.

Finally, Tarek the Bloodan, thought. Whether it was his thoughts or the Bloodan inside him thinking it, he didn't know. Regardless, someone was coming. *Man or monster, take me down. I don't deserve to exist, not in life nor in death. Kill me . . .*

Up ahead, a shadow against the smoke. It looked like a man, but was it? Perhaps. Wait. Yes, it was. There was no mistaking that tall frame with a large build and a cape as smooth as night hanging off his back. And there, beside it, something smaller. Something beautiful. Curves and . . . oh, a woman.

Woman. Woman . . . Mary. Was it her? He stopped gliding along the ground and waited for the newcomers to come into full light. He again cursed himself because it was so hard to see with only murky, red vision. It was like looking through blood-covered stained glass.

The figures neared and, yes, it was Mary. Sweet Mary. How he had betrayed her by becoming the thing—the *things*—that brought her to this place, this time of war. And the person beside her . . . . *No, it can't be. It can't. It* . . . But it was.

The Bloodan was looking at himself, looking at the man he once was.

The Bloodan-Tarek stood his ground and waited for Mary and *himself* to approach. He relaxed his body and let a liquid red cape slide down his back and hang at his ankles. He also formed red boot cuffs beneath his knees. The man drew near and had his gauntlet poised at the Bloodan's head.

"I didn't sense him approach," Bloodan-Tarek heard the man tell Mary.

"That's because" —Mary's eyes widened when she, seemingly, recognized who stood before them— "it's . . . it's you. That has to be it."

The man came right up to Bloodan-Tarek, the gauntlet never lowering. His blue eyes worked him up and down with not only puzzlement, but also disgust creasing his face.

"Name yourself," the man said.

Bloodan-Tarek couldn't believe who was before him. Just moments ago he wished a Veil would open up and he could stop himself from taking Salch. Now this man, the man he used to be, was standing before him.

"Tareksh," he replied.

The man grabbed Bloodan-Tarek, his hand sinking into Bloodan-Tarek's shoulder. The gauntlet was right up against his temple.

"You can't be me," the man said.

But I am. "I'mss . . . I'mss sshorrysh. I failedsh meesh . . . ush . . . yoosh." *Forgive me.*

The man released him—and with considerable effort, judging by the look on his face. Bloodan-Tarek immediately felt the absence of the man's hand from his body. Already he found himself reaching for the man, wanting to feel that tingle of excitement before merging with him.

In an instant, Bloodan-Tarek saw the man was about to fire. He ducked and slid between the man's legs like a liquid snake and gathered himself up behind him. The man spun, gauntlet still pointed between Bloodan-Tarek's eyes.

"Waitsh! Don'tsh kills meesh!" Was he begging for his life? Not long ago he wanted to die.

It was too late.

Blue fire swallowed him.

His body shattered and each piece of him that went flying, he knew where they were. One, over to the right, some twenty feet away. Another just behind him and off to the side, six and a half feet away. There were some in front, some to his left, even some beneath him and others shot toward the sky and were still on their way back down.

He relaxed, focused, imagined himself in his mind's eye. But the only image he saw was himself as a man. He tried to remember the Bloodan, tried and tried hard. *Remember or you're dead!*

He was fading away, losing consciousness—dying. Then, a red, shadowy figure filling his mind, saw himself as a Bloodan and slowly the liquid red pools and droplets that were once himself began to regroup and reform into a red semblance of a man.

Bloodan-Tarek stood.

As blue fire turned his vision purple and his liquid body began to boil, the last thing he heard was Mary's scream.

Chapter Twenty-one
The Circle

"Noooooo!" Mary ran over to the man— Tarek—who stood over the pool of blood that was once the Bloodan. Wildly, she beat his shoulders and chest with the heels of her fists. "Bastard! You killed him! You just killed Tarek! Don't you see? You just killed yourself. You're dead! You're dead. You're . . ." She fell against him and wept in the velvety folds of his black cape.

"I did what had to be done," he said.

"You . . . you killed him . . . you killed . . . you . . ." *Don't know how he could have done that or why. He didn't deserve that whether he was a Bloodan or not. And now I'm with Tarek, a different one, but the same one, in the end.* The soft fabric of his cape was warm against her cheeks. *Does he even realize what he's done? Does he even know?* She sniffled. *Maybe he does. Maybe it's better this way. I don't understand anymore. And I don't think I would want to, if offered the chance.*

After a time, he gently pushed her away.

"You don't know, do you?" she said.

Tarek glanced at the glistening red stain on the rocky ground. For an instant, defeat flashed across his face. "Actually, I do. We've done this before. And I've told you this before. At least half a dozen times, now. When it first started" —he took a step back from the puddle— "I didn't know what was happening, how I could be living the same sequence of events over and over again. But after the third or fourth time, I don't know, previous cycles were imprinted on me and if I focused, I understood what was going on. Furthermore, I understood what I had to do. I had to keep the cycle going, if I was to continue fighting them. I had to keep going back to Camp Silverway, keep rescuing that girl, keep meeting you and Sarah in what would be, to you, years later, keep becoming a Bloodan, keep dying by my own hand."

"But if you knew all this . . . did you just play dumb and pretend not to know who Sarah and I were? What was happening at Camp Silverway?" *I can't believe this is happening. This is so . . . so screwed up!*

"No, I didn't know. At least, when I met you and Sarah . . . when I *meet* you and Sarah, I won't know. Like I said, to know what's happening, to recognize the cycle, I have to focus on it, consciously keep it active in my mind when I return through the Veil from the Camp Silverway of long ago. But, as the moments pass I'll forget, slowly, surely, the memory of having done it all before slipping away until it will be as though I am doing everything for the first time. Here, in this world, in my Time Period, the memory lingers strong. Because of their presence here, because of how many of them there are, and because of their influence on the Veil. Their very stink is on the air. Yet going back to help you . . . your Time erases mine when I'm there, and takes away the knowledge that I'm trapped in a circle of occurrences. Or, so it's been thus far."

"Then why keep doing it? It's useless. You'll die every time. You'll kill yourself!" She did not get it and, she thought, neither did he.

He glanced up at the sky during this red dark night, and when his gaze settled back on her, his eyes looked like those of a man who had been broken a thousand times over, ten thousand times over. "I keep doing this, or *want* to keep doing this, to fight them. If I don't, they win. If I participate, then I'm at least helping humanity survive. I'm hoping that, during one of the cycles, something will be revealed to me. I'm hoping to find a means of breaking the circle and, in the end, not killing myself. I haven't found a way yet. And, for the circle to begin anew, I have to die." He put a hand on her shoulder. "There's something we must do."

Chapter Twenty-two
Lest You Forget

THE TREK BACK to where they were "supposed to go" took longer than expected. Bloodans came upon them then fell—all from fire dealt by Tarek's gauntlet— slowing their journey.

The smoke swirled about them in thick mists, the blood-red sky beating down on them glowed, like the nimbus of a moon.

"I don't know how you could live here," Mary said, "it being dark all the time. The sky's never blue, is it?"

"I have never seen a blue sky," Tarek said, "not once. Maybe I will sometime, but . . . . No, no I haven't."

You will, Tarek, Mary thought. *You'll come to Camp Silverway, when twenty-two years have passed. Passed for me, anyway. Who knows how long it'll be for you here before you return. Probably soon. You didn't look any older when I saw you next.* A paralyzing thought struck her. If Tarek didn't get any older between visits, that meant "soon" really meant *soon.* Something would happen, something that would provide a doorway back to Camp Silverway in the year 2004.

Mary crossed her fingers, not wanting to be around when that event occurred. She had already been through too much already.

Three Bloodans appeared out of the smoke, one in front and one on either side, slightly behind the first. Tarek wrapped Mary in his cape and fired off a shot at the approaching Bloodan. Inside the darkness of his cape, Mary heard the Bloodan scream as blue fire tore it apart followed by the sound of the gauntlet powering-up again.

He moved in circles, avoiding the other two creatures as they tried to take them down. Mary tried desperately to keep up, knowing that one misstep would make her trip over her own feet, or Tarek's feet, and a Bloodan would be upon her—upon them.

How long does it take for that thing to— Before she could finish her thought, a roar of flame fired from the gauntlet and another Bloodan screeched.

By now, she knew that the Bloodan first hit would be back together again and coming for them.

Tarek moved as if dancing, Mary barely catching up to his steps before he would move again. She felt safe inside his cape, like a shield, protecting her from those monsters on the other side of the fabric.

Fire roared. So did Tarek, and the dance continued until the three Bloodans were no more than red stains on the rocky earth beneath their feet. He then removed the cape from over Mary's shoulders and head.

"Are you all right?" he asked.

She was still catching her breath. Sticky sweat clung her dirty, white T-shirt to her back. "Fine. Just . . . give me a sec . . . a second."

"No time," he said and took her by the arm, leading her back in the direction they were going before the Bloodans showed up.

They went on for a good while and as they descended a rocky slope, he turned to her. "Why are you following me?"

What? What does he— "Because you told me to."

He furrowed his brow a moment. "That's right. I'm sorry. I'm beginning to forget already. By the time we reach my cave, I suspect I won't know who you are."

Oh great, she thought. "Then what? Will you take me indoors or leave me to die?"

His gaze softened. "What do you think?"

She threw her hands in the air and walked past him. "I honestly don't know."

He followed her.

Slowly, Tarek began to feel detached from himself, as though a part of his mind was slipping away. He could even picture it in his imagination: a foggy-looking white U turned on its side against a matte of black. The curve of the U pinched together and became a V, and was swept away into the chaotic black cloud that had sprung from out of nowhere and gobbled it up.

I have to remind myself to be careful next time I go through one of those . . . Veils, he thought. His arms were sore and his shoulders still ached due to the kickback from his gauntlet. Handling the weapon always commanded great strength and the device was seldom used for more than a minute; he used it for five. *Didn't expect so many Bloodans when I came ba—I wonder how the night will pan out? Hopefully, I'll be safe.* There was someone behind him. He spun around. "Who are you?"

Mary stopped in her tracks. "Don't do this, Tarek. I need you to remember me. My name is Mary, remember? Mary Thompson?"

Mary Thom—Wait. She does look familiar. Sort of. The white, foggy U appeared before his vision again, then turned to a V, and was sucked away in a swirl of charcoal black. "No." Then, almost as if someone else was saying it, "Yes. I forgot again." The U returned. For now. "I'm sorry."

"Good. Are we almost there?"

"It's just over here."

He led her around a bend at the bottom of the slope and up to the base of a large, rocky hill. He told her to stay where she was and, with ease, climbed up a few feet. Out of a hidden pouch on his belt, he withdrew a steel key then grabbed a large rock before him, no bigger than a child's head, and opened it like a door. The rock swiveled on a hinge, revealing an iron keyhole against a slab of gray metal. He stuck the key in the lock and turned it. With a hard pull, he tugged on the key and a secret door made of several rocks opened upward. Waiving his hand for Mary to follow, he went inside.

The moment his boots touched the stone inside the cavern, he heard her scream.

The U came and bent into a V and vanished quickly into black fog.

"What's going on! Who's out there?" he shouted. He grabbed either side of the hole's rim and pulled himself up just enough to peek over the rock's edge and see who screamed.

He was shocked to see a woman scrambling up the rocky hill toward him, a large pack of Bloodans on her tail.

Why wasn't he moving to help her? Why did he just stay like that, his head poking out of the hole in the hill like a gofer?

"Tarek! Help me!" Mary screamed. She glanced over her shoulder. There had to be at least thirty Bloodans right behind her.

Tarek remained motionless for a moment more, and then sprang into action.

Blue flame mixed with the red hue the sky put on everything, and for an instant, everything turned purple. Then all was red again; a Bloodan screamed.

One grabbed Mary's leg. Another jumped on top of Tarek.

Chapter Twenty-three
The Veil Opens Again

SHE GLANCED DOWN into the face of the one who held her. It was as though she had died, her heart stopping, her mind leaving her body and focusing solely on one thing: Shelly. The teen's features shimmered across the Bloodan's face like ripples in a pond: blonde hair, blue eyes, skin so fair it might as well have been white. Shelly's eyes drooped slightly at their edges, sad-like, as though she was at a funeral.

Mary's mind snapped back to the present, suddenly aware of the here-and-now. *But Shelly's alive,* she thought. *She is. I saw him save her.*

Time still did not move and Mary's mind traveled outward again, focusing on the Bloodan. Then her mind came back to her and launched her back to Cabin Seven. *How is Shelly here? I . . . . No, can't be her. The Bloodan's playing tricks on me. Don't believe it.* Tears welled in Mary's eyes. She was so detached, she didn't feel the hard grip on her ankle. *It's not possible.* Then, as though her own voice echoing from the bottom of a cave, *Taaaarrrreeekkk.*

Tarek.

Mary saw a Bloodan on top of him. Another was about to land on his head but was blown off by a bright, blue fireball. Strangely, there was no sound.

Her ears hummed with silence, like after listening to her stereo too loud.

Shelly. Poor girl. Not dead, yet not alive; somehow *imprinted* on the Bloodan that now held Mary's calve.

Mary's mind jumped out again and didn't return. She was lost to the abyss of Time and Death and Red. The aching presence of Bloodans filled her soul and a burst of blue shone briefly above her head, somewhere in the back of her mind.

Red.

Red.

Red.

Blood.

Red.

Blood.

Heat.

Slime.

Red.

Goo.

Red.

Red.

Blood.

Bloodan.

Time went away.

Tarek called out as he watched a Bloodan sink its way into Mary. He fired off another ball of flame and the one on top of him, its slick fingers finding its way between the threads in his shirt, licking his skin, flew back and splattered into a red rainstorm.

His gauntlet powered up and he aimed it at the one halfway into Mary. Then another one rose up beside him, the one he had just blown away.

He didn't know what to do. If he didn't destroy the Bloodan taking Mary, she would die. If he didn't kill the one beside him, he would die, and Mary would die anyway. He didn't have a choice.

"I'm sorry, Mary," Tarek said and turned to the one on his right. He fired and the Bloodan screeched as it tore apart into thousands of sticky droplets.

More appeared out of the smoke surrounding them. The Bloodan on top of Mary was gone, having submerged into her completely. Mary lay lifeless, her skin turning a pinky-red, as though sun-burnt.

She's dead. No. An odd feeling, kind of like déjà vu, came over him. *But it has to be this way, doesn't it? What has to be* what *way?*

A floating red dot faded into existence and slowly grew into a spinning red disc that floated horizontally to the ground. The Bloodans around it screamed, worshipping it like a god.

Mary got to her feet, her body transforming from woman to Bloodan as she rose to stand. Her red, liquid form was beautiful. Sleek, slick, utterly feminine. She joined the other Bloodans as they gathered around the disc. The disc turned itself so it was upright, a doorway, then narrowed in on itself into a red slit in the air.

Camp Silverway came into view. It looked different from how Tarek remembered it, seeming somehow . . . newer. Maybe it was the way the blue sky brightened everything, the light gray gravel on the ground, the rich brown of the wood of the lodge, the luscious green of the forest.

Suddenly becoming silent, the Bloodans stood away from the slit. Then one went through and Tarek chased it, hoping the others wouldn't follow.

Chapter Twenty-four

The Grand Repeat

*I*T WAS HAPPENING *again . . .*

Mary lay beneath the Bloodan, watching and feeling it as it seeped into her. Tarek was somewhere behind her. Or was he to the side? At her feet? She didn't know. Red was all she knew and a heat like hot bathwater as it sank its way in further.

Shelly, she thought and for some reason the thought felt *new.* "How—" Her voice was cut off as the Bloodan dribbled its way into her mouth and down her throat, occupying her esophagus, her stomach, her intestines.

Then she was lost.

It was happening again . . .

The Bloodan found its way into her. The name "Shelly" pounded in Mary's head like the beat of a drum. Then she forgot Shelly's name altogether.

There was someone else with her, she knew. She thought the person might be male, but the idea that the person was female was also possible.

Tarry.

Shelek.

Tarek and Shelly.

Shelly and Tarek.

Who were they?

The Bloodan entered her.

It was happening again . . .

Warm goo slipped and slithered through her insides like a warm cup of tea. For a moment, Mary thought of her favorite flavor: Red Rose.

Someone behind her said, "I'm sorry, Mary."
Mary . . .

It was happening again . . .
I've done this before, she thought. *Someone's behind me.* She didn't know who though. The thought left her when her soul screamed as the Bloodan took her.

In a haze of red, there was a flash and everything became purple.

Somewhere, somehow, some way—something was happening again. The eerie presence of déjà vu knocked on the door to Mary's heart.

Don't forget about me, she thought. "Remember, please . . ." she said. "Save me."

"Hi, Mary." It was Shelly. Mary would recognize that voice anywhere. It was the same voice she heard in her head since the summer of . . . how long ago was that, again? A high voice, like that of a child no more than six. When the voice spoke again, it was low and garbled. "Remembersh meesh?"

Mary tried to scream and someone apologized to her. Or was it to Shelly? Did she herself just apologize to someone?

Purple.

Red.

Nothing.

Over and over again. Over and over, time and again.

Red. Blood. Purple.

The moments all merged into one.

"I've got you," someone said. It sounded female.

"I've got you," someone said. It sounded male.

The moments merged again.

Merge. That sounded familiar.

Water surrounded her. Something was *off*—different.

"I'm sorry, Mary." It was a man.

She slipped away.

Merge.

Shelly.

"I'm sorry, Mary," Tarek said.

"I've got you," he said soon after.

"I've gotsh yoush," Shelly said. Her speech was low, slurred and garbled.

Mary screamed.

Then died.

Then became . . .

Mary dog-paddled in circles in a red lake, where she knew she wasn't supposed to be. The water was pleasantly warm on her skin, the air smelling salty and . . . absent? That wasn't right either, but the air certainly was not alive. Nor was it dead. It just seemed *away*. Too *still* to even exist.

The sky was blood-red, dotted with black clouds. Bright red droplets began to rain down on her the moment she glanced up at it.

Something grabbed her ankle, a sharp pinch against her skin, and Mary was sure that whatever just grabbed her had dug its claws straight through her flesh and bone and clear to the other side. The red lake swirled above her in a funnel as she was pulled down. No air bubbles came from her mouth when she screamed. No air came either.

"I got you," a man said.

A flash of purple flickered and its light suddenly turned blue.

A man she did not recognize was on his knees beside her, his palm on her forehead.

Chapter Twenty-five
Tarek and the Circle

T HE CYCLE HAD repeated itself: Tarek saving Shelly at Camp Silverway in 1982. Tarek leaving and returning to the camp twenty-two years later, saving Mary from one of the Bloodans that had gotten through the Veil. The return to his own Time and meeting Mary there, again, saving her from a pack of Bloodans. He meeting himself—a Bloodan-version of himself—and killing it. Ending his own life, never giving in to his fate. There was the final struggle with the Bloodans, Mary consumed by one as another Veil opened up to a cleaner-looking, daytime version of Camp Silverway. Tarek running into the past for the umpteenth time.

The cycle began again. And again. And again. Each time Tarek went through the cycle of events, the more he was able to remember from the events previous. To a small extent, anyway. He was only able to recall most vividly his first time at Camp Silverway and most of what went on in his own Time Period. Much of what happened while in the past disappeared into forgotten memory, especially him becoming a Bloodan. The only time he was aware of his doom was when he encountered himself in his own Time and, as always, killed himself.

However, with each pass through the cycle, the more *aware* of it he became. He knew that he, along with Mary and all the others involved, were locked into a pattern of some sort and there was no choice but to see the cycle through to its end, so it could begin anew. Yet, he wanted out of the cycle. He remembered killing the Bloodan-version of himself and the hurt in his heart when he did so, the anguishing pain of knowing he would become the enemy.

There had to be a way out.

It would only be a matter of time before a solution would present itself, but until then, the circle had to continue.

The Bloodan that was once Sarah wandered through the smoke, seeking out another life to consume. It/she was so hungry, so thirsty, so in need of blood and satisfaction, she'd do or give anything to have the emptiness filled.

Her red form moved through the smoke like water around rocks in a river, silently, smoothly, waiting for a human to come by. She knew humans were evil. Some of her kin, the other Bloodans, had fallen to their blue flame. She had escaped just in time, barely avoiding a fireball shot at her.

Now she was alone, wandering through the smoke, following the scent of human blood. Time went on and she stopped her stride when she smelled something . . . off. There, up ahead and a little to the right. A human? No. A Bloodan? Couldn't be. Yet it smelled both familiar and foreign at the same time. Carefully, she made her way over to its source and sank down onto her knees before a blood-red stain on the rocky ground.

She sniffed again then trailed her fingers over the wet stain, the liquid of her fingertips absorbing some of the thin film of blood still on the ground. Smelling it nearly made her gag; nearly made her body give in to the blessed need of something to eat.

This was not human blood. Nor was it like her own.

She licked her fingers and savored the sweet taste of whatever this thing had been. The blood trickled down her throat and coated her insides everywhere and all over. Before she was aware of it, she was already leaning over, mere inches from the stain, about to merge with it.

The wonderful aroma of the blood tantalized her senses, repulsed her, but she let herself fall into the stain, gathering the droplets around the puddle toward her, joining with it, needing it.

Becoming it.

Tarek wasn't sure what pass of the cycle he was on, but right now, he didn't care. He fired off another burst of flame from his gauntlet. Down on the slope below him, Mary struggled beneath the crushing weight of a Bloodan soaking into her.

He was surrounded and without thinking, he moved down the hill toward her.

A blast of blue flame spewed forth from the gauntlet's tip and slammed into the Bloodan on top of Mary. The creature scattered into a thousand gooey red droplets. Tarek raced over to her and placed a hand on her forehead. She blinked her eyes open just as a couple more of the creatures rose over the hill and flew through the air toward his back. Landing on him, they drove him into the rocks, his forehead hitting a small boulder hard, breaking the skin. Stars burst before his vision and he knew the scent of blood leaking from his forehead would drive them into a frenzy, killing him in moments.

Through watery eyes, he glanced up and saw Mary sitting up, her arms raising to shield herself as the Bloodan that was just on her had put itself back together and was nearly on top of her once more. His gauntlet powered up and he shot it again. This time the creature blew apart and as the blood rained around him and Mary, the two on his back began to seep into him.

All seemed lost. He tried to turn himself over and fire another round, but he couldn't move. They weren't heavy, but what weight they had by their attempt to merge with him kept him pinned to the ground.

"Mary . . ." he said into the stone pressed up against his face.

There was the sound of footsteps and then a female voice calling his name.

"Mary," he said again.

"Tarek," she said.

He felt her near him; her slim fingers touched his head. The Bloodan on top of him screeched and jerked forward. Mary's touch vanished. Though he couldn't see what happened, he presumed the creature had knocked Mary backward.

The Bloodan at his back began digging into him again, merging with him.

Then something started pulling the Bloodans away.

Chapter Twenty-six
The Unexpected Pairing

THE BLOODANS WERE so deep within him that pulling them away felt as if someone was ripping out his spine. Tarek shook when the last of the Bloodans syrupy tendrils left him. He lay face down on the rock, gasping, a part of him anticipating another attack.

Just roll over and start firing. Have to move. Have to get up. He forced himself onto his back. He laid there, gauntlet poised, expecting to see Bloodans looming over him. Instead, there was nothing save wisps of smoke from the battleground and the red sky high above.

A Bloodan screeched behind him, half its tone low and droning like a growl, the other half high-pitched like a woman's scream.

"Something's not right," he said and got to his feet.

As a Bloodan scampered up the hill toward him, he fired off a shot and it blew apart. However, it was the one at the very bottom of the hill, the one drawing the other Bloodans away from him that held his attention.

This one, the one at the bottom, was large, probably at least seven feet tall. It appeared to be a female, with a well-muscled, liquid, red frame and a long gooey cape hanging from her shoulders like a shawl.

Mary screeched and Tarek shot one of them grabbing her arm. The one he had first shot, the one that had run up the hill toward him, gathered itself and joined its kin at the bottom. The same went for the one that grabbed Mary after re-forming.

Bloodans raced from all over: from behind the hill, from the hovering clouds of smoke along the ground, and the ones that were already near the big Bloodan slid their feet along the ground even closer.

"Mary!" Tarek shouted as he made his way over to her.

When the two met, the big female Bloodan at the bottom screamed a low, droning growl coupled with a high-pitched feminine-sounding scream. The female Bloodan squatted down and the others surrounding her jumped on top of her like a bunch of football players in a pile-up. In a blast of red aggression, the big Bloodan threw the others off and she bounded into the air like a bird taking flight. There was no telling how far her arc through the smoky clouds would take her. She was gone from view, lost to the smoke around and above them, before Tarek could acknowledge what just happened.

I don't understand.

"Come on, let's go," he told Mary and took her by the hand.

"What was that?" she asked.

"Don't know. Don't care. Let's go!"

They ran down the hill, around its middle and descended on its opposite side. The Bloodans on the other side of the hill screeched and howled and instead of chasing them as he thought they would, they didn't follow. Where they went or if they had gone completely, he didn't care. He just wanted to leave and take Mary as far away as possible.

She seemed to agree with his feelings because she squeezed his hand tighter as they began to sprint. Tarek dug his heels into the rocky ground to keep up and the two disappeared into the smoke-filled air.

They were far away from the hill or, at least, Mary thought so. Her lungs burned with the need for air and the smoke all around wasn't helping. Tarek didn't seem to be out of breath one bit, but she could tell she was the faster runner of the two.

Thighs burning, she suddenly remembered how tired she was. She hadn't eaten or slept in what had to be at least twenty hours, if not more. She was a lover of sleep. At least, on the nights she didn't dream about the summer of '82. But now, after having been so *into* the reality of the Bloodans, Tarek, and this war he—even she—was involved in, the memory of what happened in 1982 didn't seem nearly as bad.

She swallowed; a dry lump scraped along the back lining of her throat. "Can we . . . can we stop?" she asked, panting.

Tarek waved his gauntlet in front of him slowly from left to right. He didn't respond but instead merely slowed their pace until they were both walking briskly.

Her lungs pounded and sour spit filled her mouth. She stopped, put her hands on her knees, her head between them, and spat, watching as her saliva mixed in with the dust on the ground, forming a browny-gray sludge.

Tarek, a few paces in front, turned to her. "This is no time to stop. They're everywhere."

"I know," she said, "just . . . just gimme . . . a sec."

Having been able to slow down felt so wonderful and Mary wished she could curl up in a ball and fall asleep. Her eyelids felt noticeably heavier as fatigue began to take hold.

"Come on," Tarek said, suddenly at her side. He gently took her by the arm and the two began to walk quickly.

"Sorry," she said, "I'm not used to this."

"It's okay," he said. "We'll have plenty of time to rest once we find a safe place to hide."

"What about another Shelter?"

"The one we were just at, it was the last one in my sector. It was the farthest one on the border between my section and Rurt's. I don't know his area as well as I should and that's where we are now." Sadness filled his eyes.

"What's wrong?"

"I think we're lost," he said.

Those were the last words she expected to hear. To her, he was invincible. She always thought he knew exactly what was going on and what to do when things got difficult, even impossible. He saved her from Bloodans, after all. Not just once but several times. A person who did not know what they were doing wouldn't be able to come through the way he had on so many occasions.

But he did fall, didn't he? she thought. *A Bloodan took him. Or a version of him, anyway. I wonder where the* other *Tarek is, if he still even exists. Was—* "—the cycle ended?" she finished aloud.

"Cycle?" Tarek looked confused. Then a knowing expression crossed his face. "Right. I remember. Yes, I think it has."

"That's good, right?" she asked. *Of course it is, don't be stupid. Idiot.*

"Yes. It is good." He touched her shoulder and gave it a thoughtful squeeze.

"Sarah." Mary stopped walking. "Do you know where she is?"

He glanced into the smoke. "I think she fell. We would have heard something by now. Actually, we should have heard many things by now. Rurt reportedly has a vast number of men working under him. His platoon, it is said, is double—if not triple—that of most commanding officers. Most of the men in the other sectors have been killed. However, Rurt's area, thankfully, is considered somewhat of a safe zone. I'm surprised we haven't run into anybody."

She wandered a few paces ahead. Faint, dark gray shapes dotted the smoke and the further she walked, she then saw human carcasses littering the ground. He came up beside her and told her to be wary, that Bloodans could still be about.

"There's so many bodies," she said.

"Too many," he said. "I've never seen this before. I've only heard of it, supposedly back when this war started. They say you could see mounds of bodies so high they looked like walls." He surveyed the area, his gauntlet at the ready. "These are no walls, but . . . there's far too many bodies, even for the Bloodans to amass. I don't know wha—"

Up ahead, beyond a pile of at least ten bodies, a dark shape stirred in the fog. The shadow of the shape was huge, over twenty feet high, yet it grew smaller as it neared. Tarek and Mary ran to the nearest pile of corpses and hid behind them, the bodies acting as a barrier.

Mary covered her mouth, afraid to breathe so close to the dead. Their smell was awful, especially mixed with the smoke around them. Tears ran from her eyes and she couldn't believe how many dead people there were in one place.

"Stay down," Tarek said.

She nodded and slumped even further down by the bodies while he peered over the edge of a fallen soldier's blood-covered stomach, searching the gloom for anything coming toward them.

They're covered in blood, she thought, eyeing some of the bodies across from her. *But no Bloodans. They didn't join with these people. I thought Bloodans always joined with whom they killed? Absorbed them?* "Tarek?"

"Shh," he whispered. "Keep quiet."

What do I know about Bloodans, anyway? she thought. *They could probably kill someone without joining with him or her, right? Maybe there were too many people here, more than there were Bloodans and the Bloodans just jumped from person to person?*

Tarek settled back down beside her. "It's gone."

She sighed, relieved they were safe.

From around the bodies they were next to, a Bloodan slid in front of them, quick as a snake.

A microsecond later, gauntlet aimed at the creature, Tarek blasted a blue fireball into the Bloodan. The burst scattered against the ground like a water balloon hitting a brick wall, and when the fire and smoke cleared, she was stunned to see the ground was bare. No Bloodan. No red stain. No drop of blood anywhere.

Something rose up behind them and when they turned to see what it was, she screamed as the huge Bloodan on the hill of corpses stared down at them.

Tarek tried to fire his gauntlet, but it was still powering-up. The Bloodan jumped down and effortlessly knocked it off his forearm. They slowly circled each other.

And then, as though memory had suddenly become something tangible and alive, Mary saw in the liquid red face an amalgamation of Sarah and . . . Tarek?

Chapter Twenty-seven
The Veil Returns

"MARY, BE CAREFUL," Tarek said.

The large Bloodan loomed over them. Its form was female, perfect, even sensual. Smooth shoulders flowed into slender arms. Breasts, round and smooth, curved in to a small waist at the middle. Round hips that would make any girl jealous branched out, running into toned thighs and shapely calves. A short cape of blood hung limply off its shoulders. There were no boot cuffs beneath its knees, Mary noticed. Tarek, even as a Bloodan, had boot cuffs.

Silence became everything as the three stood there, each eyeing the other. Mary wondered if the Bloodan would attack them. *No, because if it wanted to, it would have by now,* she thought.

"Tarek?" she said. He set his gaze toward her but it wasn't him she was talking to. "Sarah?"

The Bloodan, faceless, emotionless, nodded its head.

Oh my . . . it's true, Mary thought. "How . . . who did this to you? How are you together? What happened?"

"Mary, what are you talking about?" Tarek asked.

She pointed at the Bloodan. "This . . . thing . . . is Sarah, is you . . . is . . . they're the same . . . together. I don't know. What's going on?"

Tarek didn't seem to understand her. He looked off to somewhere past the Bloodan, presumably to see where his gauntlet fell.

"It'sh meesh," the creature said. Its voice was like hearing two sets of words at the same time, but in opposite tones: one high and female, the other low and male.

"Sarah . . ." Mary said as she moved toward her.

She reached out to touch the Bloodan. Just as her arms were about to wrap around the Bloodan's waist, Tarek grabbed her from behind and dragged her away.

"No! What do you think you are doing?" he said. "This *thing* may be quiet now, but it will kill you."

"It won't!" she shouted. "Sarah, Tarek, please tell him it's all right."

"It'sh all rightsh, Mareesh," the Bloodan said. Swiftly, the creature moved toward Tarek and with one hand freed Mary and with the other lifted him up by the top of his head, his feet dangling two feet off the ground. "It'sh okaysh."

Though Mary couldn't be sure, she thought Tarek might have seen something in the Bloodan's face since his grimace relaxed and his eyes widened.

Maybe he saw himself? she thought.

The Bloodan set Tarek down and the moment the warrior's boots touched the ground, a swarm of Bloodans appeared out of the fog.

Tarek ran and Mary thought he was deserting her. The Bloodans came in fast and hard and jumped on the largest of their kin: the amalgamation of Sarah and Tarek.

The human-Tarek returned, his gauntlet proudly displayed on his forearm. He shot and blue fire took out two Bloodans at the same time. Their wails filled the air and their screams echoed inside Mary's head.

She frantically looked about for some place to hide. She could find none save for perhaps using the bodies around her as a barricade of some sort. For a moment, she'd almost forgotten she was in a graveyard.

Ducking as a Bloodan came at her, the creature flew over her head and landed in a splash a short few feet away. Mary ran to what appeared to be a high pile of bodies to the right. Her heart filled with warmth when she heard another roar of flame escape Tarek's gauntlet.

Sarah, she thought. Glancing over her shoulder, she saw the Bloodans surrounding Sarah-Tarek, clutching and hanging on to the Sarah-Tarek merge, their bodies absorbing together, becoming one.

"No!" Mary screamed and ran back toward the fight.

"Mary, get out of here!" Tarek shouted.

"But . . . but Sarah . . . ?"

"Is dead!"

The ground shook and several feet above their heads, a red dot faded into existence. It began to expand, soon turning into a swirling disc of blood.

The Sarah-Tarek creature roared and threw off a couple of the Bloodans.

"Sarah!" Mary screamed.

The large Bloodan glanced her way but had to turn away again when three more creatures appeared out of the smoke and dove at its legs.

A ball of fire hit a Bloodan charging toward Mary.

"I said go!" Tarek shouted.

The disc spun faster and faster, already standing upright, soon forming a slit, a doorway made of red, gooey liquid. Was it just her imagination or was this disc bigger, darker, than the others?

"It's huge," she said quietly.

As though her words triggered it, the swirling, twirling, slosh of blood that was the disc bent, rippled, shimmered, and formed a slit in the air. The veil opened to Camp Silverway.

Is it the same one? Mary wondered. *Is it the same camp I left? The same Time?* It looked like it. It wasn't night. Not like the summer of '82.

"Mary, go through it," Tarek shouted as he sidestepped a Bloodan diving at his legs and fired blue flame at another behind him.

"But—but what about you?"

He didn't answer, instead turning to meet another attack.

The Veil's rim spun even faster and the blood that bordered the doorway began flying off like batter out of a mixing bowl.

Sarah-Tarek writhed in agony as over a dozen Bloodans joined with it, merged with it. Mary saw the staunch horror on both Sarah *and* Tarek's faces.

"Leeeaavsh," the Sarah-Tarek Bloodan said as four others sprang from the cloud of smoke above, plowing her into the ground in a syrupy splash.

Heart racing, legs ready to collapse beneath her, Mary ran toward the Veil, the blood flying off it from its ever-increasing spin splashing her, getting in her eyes, her mouth, down her shirt, soaking through her pants, getting on her feet. She smeared the blood away from her eyes and through the murky red vision of blood and tears, saw Camp Silverway beginning to shimmer and roll, like water coming into shore.

Go. Just jump. Dive. Anything! she thought.

The roar of flame echoed behind her as the Sarah-Tarek Bloodan screamed its last.

Mary jumped through the doorway just as it began to fade from view. Bloodans chased after her but the Veil had already shrunk too small for them to get through.

Chapter Twenty-eight
Try and Remember

Wɪᴛʜ ᴀ ʀᴇᴅ flash, a warm wind blew Mary backward into the dark. She braced for impact, to hit the grassy ground at Camp Silverway. Instead, she crashed into the woman's body hard and quick. When her back landed on the woman's chest and abdomen, it was like falling backward onto a thin mattress with rough concrete underneath. She gasped the moment she hit. She tried to sit up, to see what she had landed against, but it was too dark to see anything. From either side of her the woman's arms embraced her, giving her a strong hug from behind. The woman squeezed harder and harder until Mary felt herself going *into* the woman.

Almost like how it felt when the Bloodan was sinking into me, she thought, *but backwards.*

She tried to shake herself free but the more she struggled, the harder the woman pulled her in. It had to be a woman, she knew. A man's arms wouldn't be as thin as this and his skin wouldn't be as soft and smooth.

The woman drew her in deeper and deeper. Soon she stopped struggling and the woman took her in all the way.

Tightly gripping her quilt, Mary gasped again and sat up in bed. Sweat trickled down her back. The room was a bit brighter, not nearly as dark as before. Watery moonlight seeped in through the thin cracks in the blinds behind her. She put her fingers to her temples and massaged her head.

So cold, she thought. *I'm freezing!*

Then, beside her, heavy breathing, and, "Hmh." It was a man's voice.

Slowly, Mary felt her way across the sheets to the warm body beside her. She jerked her hand back when she realized she was in bed next to a person. Shivering, she jumped out of bed and turned on the light by the door.

How did I know the light was here? she wondered. *Where am I? What's—*

"Honey, what's wrong?" the man asked.

As her eyes adjusted to the light, Mary saw that the man was Doug. He was alive! *How did you survive . . . . That was a long time ago, wasn't it?* She wasn't sure though. Camp Silverway and the attack of the Bloodans seemed so recent, so near. Yet it also seemed like something further away, something that happened years past.

"Nothing," she said. She shivered again. "Just . . . cold."

"Oh. Well, change into something warmer and come back to bed." Doug glanced at the clock on the night table. "It's nearly four. I gotta get up at six." His head dropped to the pillow.

"Sorry," she said and turned off the light.

"S'okay." The sheets rustled as Doug rolled over, facing away from her.

Mary knew he was already asleep. He always fell asleep fast and hated waking in the middle of the night. She didn't know how she knew it; she just did.

She left the room and went downstairs, her hand instinctively finding the rail in the dark. For a second she thought she had kids, then remembered she and Doug had only been married for a year, and wanted to have at least two or three years to themselves before any kids came along.

At the bottom of the stairs, she turned right and entered the living room, and flicked on the light. An ornate wooden dining table sat in the middle of the room, ringed with soft-looking chairs. Beside the table was a china cabinet filled with all sorts of white plates, cups, chalices and bright silver cutlery. The tiny teaspoons were her favorite, she remembered.

The bookshelf sat beside the china cabinet and on top of it, their wedding pictures. She went over to them and held the biggest of the four pictures on display.

We're not married, she thought. *Doug died at Camp Silverway. I was there. The blood.* Her eyes widened. *Bloodans. Tarek. Sarah.*

But there Sarah was, her Maid of Honor, in the picture alongside her and Doug, and to Doug's right, his younger brother, Steve, who was the Best Man. It was just the four of them in that picture, the photo taken outside St. Mary's Cathedral on a cloudy day. It had rained from just before the reception started right until the next morning when she and Doug were on a plane to Barbados for their honeymoon.

Tarek, she thought. *Bloodans. Where am I?*

There was a mirror in the front landing and when Mary looked into it, she jumped back at her reflection. She looked different. Her skin was smooth and fair, and didn't look so *used* from years of reliving the summer of '82. Her brown hair was shorter, hanging down only to her jaw line instead of to her shoulders.

1982, Mary thought. *It did happen. It's so clear in my head and—* "I remember," she said. "But I dealt with it years ago. Made peace with it. Doug helped me. Sarah, too. I even talked to Shelly last month to see how she was doing and, for the umpteenth time, reminded myself she was alive and well." *Shelly remembers that summer, too, but tries not to think about it.* "A couple of years ago, right before Doug proposed to me, I went to Camp Silverway for the last time. Faced the past. It had been a terrific summer." *Too bad I'm no longer a counselor.*

Mary walked through the entire house, taking in each room, reliving the memories each brought, memories of her and Doug in those rooms, memories that seemed real but ones she was sure never happened. Yet by the time she returned to the master bedroom and crawled into bed next to him, thoughts of Tarek and the Bloodans and Camp Silverway were more reminisces of a dream.

Before nodding off to sleep, she recalled falling backward into a woman, the woman holding her, drawing her in. The woman, she later realized, was *herself.* It was as if she finally caught up with herself, finally caught up with the future and was able to let the past go.

For the first time she could recall, she fell asleep peacefully.

Epilogue
Thunder

T EN YEARS LATER, what happened to Shelly so long ago, Mary hardly ever gave it thought. Now and again, she would remember sitting high up on that bunk bed, her face in her hands, and tears in her eyes. There was something about a flash of blue and a scream, but beyond that, there was nothing. Nothing to do with that nightmare past at all. Those memories were replaced by full days working as a secretary in the same office as Doug, evenings taking the kids to swimming lessons, baseball, recitals. Even their dog, Bobbo, was in there somewhere.

Doug and the kids were out for the evening and Mary was alone, cleaning up the kitchen after meatballs and rice for dinner. Tonight, she was going to relax, do nothing and watch some TV.

As she placed a plate in the dishwasher, the crash of broken glass came from upstairs.

Mary jumped.

Okay, okay, don't panic. It's all right. She didn't know if she should check to see what it was or call the police. It might be a burglar.

Just check. If you hear anything else, call the cops. She quietly finished setting the plate in the dishwasher and slowly, stepping cautiously, made her way upstairs.

At the top, the main hallway was dark. No light seeped in from the cracks underneath the closed doors on either side. The bathroom door was open and it was dark inside there as well.

Mary's ears perked up when she heard footsteps on the carpet to her right, behind the door.

Someone was *inside* her room.

Her heart sped, thundering almost mercilessly inside her chest. She put her hand upon her breast to try to calm it down, but to no success.

She debated for a moment to return downstairs to the kitchen and dial the police.

WhatdoIdo? WhatdoIdo? How she wished Doug was here.

The footsteps on the carpet resumed, and they weren't *Doug's* footsteps. She had always been able to tell where he was in the house just by listening to the weight of his footsteps on the floor, causing the floorboards beneath the carpet to creak.

The footsteps she heard now were heavier, carrying more authority, as whoever was making them had some business here.

Just call the police, she thought. She turned to go down the stairs, her hand already reaching for the railing.

Behind her, a door opened. A shudder raced up her back and her neck muscles locked. Her palms became instantly sweaty.

With a yelp, she ran down the stairs.

Skidding to a stop before the phone on the kitchen's slippery tiles, she nearly lost her balance, luckily grabbing the chair next to the phone to keep herself from falling. The chair teetered on its legs, but did not fall. In a short second, a loud *thunk* vibrated the floor and the person who opened the door was at the bottom of the stairs.

They jumped from the top step. That's eight stairs! she thought. She grabbed the phone and for the first time in her life found it hard to find the numbers she wanted on the keypad. *911, that's all. Okay, slow down. 9-1-1. Come on!*

The figure moved out of the dark and the phone dropped from Mary's hands when she saw who it was.

Tarek.

No! He's not real! her mind screamed. She vaguely recalled him from the summer of '82, but he was no more of a memory than the strands of brown hair hanging over her eyes when she had been crying, sitting on the top bunk.

"Mary. It's okay. It's me," he said.

"Nononononono." Her words slurred together and her mouth became uncomfortably dry. "You're—you're not real. You're . . . no, you can't be. No . . . ."

He took a step closer and she took a step back. Tarek looked somehow . . . different. Gray streaked his brown hair, his hair shorter than what she thought it should be. The black cape held to his back by a leather strap across his chest looked worn and soft, like a well-used blanket. His boots were scuffed and any shine they once had was lost long ago. Beneath his white shirt with the flared-out cuffs, his frame was thinner, at least fifty pounds less than what she thought he should be.

How do I know this? He's . . . . No, long gone. Wake up, you're dreaming. She bent down to pick up the phone. The dial tone played a monotonous beep after having been off the hook for too long. Before she could replace the phone in its cradle, Tarek was at her side, her hand with the phone suddenly caught by his fingers.

"I need your help," he said.

Tarek came in through the upstairs window, he told Mary, because he didn't want to be seen by anyone. He had rounded the back of the house, where the only two windows were from the top two bedrooms on the second floor. He climbed up the vine ladder between the windows then used his gauntlet to break the glass that belonged to the master bedroom.

"But why are you here?" Mary asked.

"Like I said, I need your help."

Need my help? With what? "Look, I've spent the better part of my life trying to forget what happened at Camp Silverway. I was only a kid when that girl—See? I can't even remember her name. Started with an S though. Regardless, no more. I'm done with it. I just want to be left alone."

They sat in the front room; he was on Doug's recliner, yet sitting up, alert. She was on the black leather loveseat across from him. Tarek had his gauntlet in his lap, stroking it as though it was a pussycat. He leaned forward slightly and told her of what happened a dozen years ago, about the both of them ending something that kept occurring. Unfortunately, he said he couldn't remember what that "something" was. He just knew they had set something right.

What's he talking about? She couldn't remember any of it. "Look, what do you want from me? I don't want to be a part of this." She glanced out the window, hoping to see Doug and the kids pull up into the driveway in the station wagon.

The moment the rumble hit, Mary jumped to her feet and so did Tarek. The low growling, seeming to come from the very air around her, surged through her every bone.

The glass doors that sealed off the fireplace from the rest of the living room shook, rattled. As Tarek led her away, she found herself unable to breathe.

Thick globs of blood seeped through the cracks in between the doors' tiny frames, dripping over and around the glass like a waterfall in slow motion. It pooled on the stone ledge before the fireplace.

A machine-like powering-up sound came from Tarek's gauntlet and a flush of relief came over Mary. She had never known something to sound so good. *Yet I have, haven't I?* she thought.

The pool of thick blood gathered into a moving bubble and, soon after, took on a humanlike shape.

A sudden blue flash burned Mary's eyes.

About the Author

A.P. Fuchs is the author of many novels and short stories, most of which have been published. His most recent books are the first three installments in the *Blood of my World* vampire series: *Discovery of Death, Memories of Death, Life of Death.* He's also author of the zombie novels, *Possession of the Dead* and *Zombie Fight Night: Battles of the Dead,* in which zombies fight such classic monsters as werewolves, vampires, Bigfoot, and even go up against awesome foes like pirates, ninjas, and . . . Bruce Lee.

A.P. Fuchs is also known for his superhero series, *The Axiom-man Saga,* and the author of the shoot 'em up zombie trilogy, *Undead World.* He also edited the zombie anthologies *Dead Science* and *Vicious Verses and Reanimated Rhymes: Zany Zombie Poetry for the Undead Head.*

Fuchs lives and writes in Winnipeg, Manitoba.

Visit his corner of the Web at
www.canisterx.com

Follow him on Twitter at
www.twitter.com/ap_fuchs

More from the World of
A.P. FUCHS
WWW.CANISTERX.COM